Jennifer Roan

By Matthew Lee

Sometimes you don't realize something is a problem until it bites you on the ass. My girlfriend, Jennifer, and I live in Madison, Wisconsin, attending the university there. We are both on athletic scholarships; for her gymnastics and for me, baseball. We have our own apartments but lately she stays more with me.

The problem I mentioned is this town has only two costume shops. No big deal, usually, but that does cause some duplication at costume parties, like this one, and I found myself staring across the room at an identical Marc Antony. No matter, his date was nowhere near as hot as mine. He was more muscled than me, like a football player, but our costumes matched perfectly.

Last year the frat threw this party in a dorm on campus and caused a lot of problems. This year they used one of the quaint two-story red-brick homes not far from school. At least all the trees and dense foliage muffled the music. Most of the neighbors are students too and never complain, but just in case something did go wrong, this year they told everyone to wear small black masks too.

Outside was cold and windy but inside we roasted. Both heaters roared at full strength and add to that a hundred young bodies and the temperature had to be close to a hundred. Even in a skirt I still sweat. Jennifer was perfectly comfortable. Her costume consisted of a diaphanous black lace gown with strategically placed double layers. The rest of her costume was mostly jewelry and make-up, including lots of body paint. She looked sexy as hell. The nipples which topped her baseball-sized breasts had been visible in the bright light of the seven-eleven, but the house was dimly lit so one had to stare to see them, and plenty of guys did. In fact, the house was dark enough I'd already walked into walls, twice, and I'd not really had that much to drink yet.

Jennifer had but oddly she is always able to hold her liquor better than me. Practice, I guess. We danced some and chatted with friends some and even smoked a little weed. Jen grew hornier by the second because that's what booze and weed does to her. It mostly makes me sleepy so I'd already cut back.

Jen finished her beer and asked if I wanted another. I declined. She left me leaning against the speakers to head for the tub in the kitchen packed with ice and Corona.

My friend Brian walked around the corner and we talked for a minute before he asked if I'd seen Shelia's costume. I hadn't. Shelia is a cheerleader for the Badgers and a gorgeous one. She also loves sex and almost all of my friends enjoyed her this semester. He tugged my arm and told me I had to get a look at her, so I followed.

He was right; Shelia was something to see. She was Poison Ivy from DC Comics, but aside from the long red wig, her costume was literally painted on. Even in that dim light I made out nipples and labia. Shelia stood nude in front of the student body and did not give a fuck. Drama majors, right?

It all worked though. She totally pulled it off. She looked perfect. Her costume was flawless down to the last vine and leaf. Best of all, at the moment she made out with Jayne, a nerdy political science girl who was dressed as Harley Quinn and looked stunning too. Jayne is shy and quiet and Shelia had her pinned to the wall and her tongue wiggling in Jayne's mouth. Instant heat lit up my crotch. A circle of voyeurs formed, male and female, and all of us just stared appreciatively. Tomorrow Jayne would probably regret this moment, but for now the hottest girl in school wanted her and she rolled with it.

Brian looked at me like he had the answer sheet to our physics final.

The two girls kept escalating things until Shelia pushed a finger up Jayne's pussy. That snapped her out of it and she grabbed Shelia's wrist and headed for a bedroom. A wave of disappointment swept the crowd. Brian and I talked a bit longer and then he went to look for some girl to take his sexual frustration out on. By the look of the crowd, he'd have no trouble finding one.

My foggy brain remembered Jennifer and I returned to my spot by the speakers, looking for her. She wasn't there. In fact, she wasn't anywhere. I searched that floor and then upstairs but did not find her. It was possible she used a restroom so I waited a bit and then searched again. I realized the only place I had not searched was the basement. I located the stairs and descended into darkness.

This area held a bar and pool table and two chairs and a couch. The only light source was a tiny blinking pink neon cat wagging its tail. Nobody shot pool but the chairs and couch held obviously stoned couples making out and more than making out.

I waited for my eyes to adjust but before they did I heard a soft feminine moan from farther back in the room where it was almost pitch-black. I wanted to see, of course, especially after Shelia and Jayne, but I didn't want to intrude. I crept forward as much as I could without getting caught, making a circle of my search.

Blurry white shapes moved in sensuous rhythm. A small female figure leaned over what looked like boxes or bins and behind her a much larger figure gently thrust in and out. Even in the low light the size of his massive penis was evident; a long and thick pale tube connected them, appearing and disappearing with smooth and steady regularity, her moans perfectly matching in time. They were lost in each other and oblivious to me so I slowed as I move by them, pretending to place my feet carefully in the dark. I drew closer and they were still unaware.

She had a great body; fit and strong, and she pushed her pussy back at him by bracing herself against the wall. His heavy cock shoved an exhale from her on each thrust, followed by a womanly moan of intense pleasure.

"Jesus, Paul," she whispered, hoarsely. "From this angle you feel huge."

I froze. The voice was Jennifer's or so close to her voice I couldn't tell the difference. Admittedly I was a little high and a little buzzed, but it sounded exactly like her, even to her use of my name. But why would my girlfriend fuck someone else? I kept walking until I reached my closet point to them.

Now I could see better. Marc Antony had Cleopatra bent over several cardboard boxes, her lace skirt pushed up over her ass, his hefty cock swinging in and out, his underwear stretched around his ankles. It was my girlfriend Jen, but it wasn't me behind her.

In the greatest mystery of my life, at least up to this point, I said nothing, I did nothing. All I could do was watch. I liked what I saw. Actually, I *loved* what I saw. Jen looked unbelievably sexy. Of course I'd never had this view of her. I'd never even imagined this view of her. Now here it was right in front of me and I felt my penis rapidly growing under my Roman legionnaire's skirt. I was a little jealous but mostly I was ferociously turned on.

Jennifer covered her head with her arms and bit her bicep. Her breathing was rapid and shallow and before I figured out what was happening, her body jerked and shook and she smothered her orgasmic cry with her arm. She was cumming! Standing up! From fucking! My dick had never made her climax, and that's from any and every angle. She loved it but to get her to orgasm I needed my tongue. Her strong legs trembled and her ass moved up and down and the guy behind her held her butt and drove her orgasm higher.

Before she'd finished hers he grunted and started his. I heard her croak, "Give me every drop, Baby." He gripped her hips and his pelvis sped up until he slammed it in one last time and held it there, balls deep, as he emptied his load of sperm, jet after jet flying out of him and into her. Even as he pumped his last spurt he reached for his underwear. He knew he needed to get the fuck out of there before he got caught.

I left before he did, in a daze, my mind doing somersaults. On the way by the kitchen I grabbed another beer. Trembling, I took my position by the speakers again. Minutes later Jen joined me, still adjusting her costume. Her face bore not one molecule of shame or regret. She leaned up and kissed my cheek.

"That was so hot, Baby. You fucked my brains out. Can you believe you made me cum like that? I'm such a bad girl. Your dick felt so big! Why'd you leave so fast? Did someone see us?"

As she spoke she discreetly took my hand and guided it under her skirt. Her pussy was sopping wet, most of it him. My fingers were bathing in another man's semen.

"I can't believe how much you came, Honey. I guess you found that as exciting as I did. Did you notice someone watching us? I think we almost got caught."

Her face was guileless.

"What makes you say that?" I asked numbly.

"I thought I saw someone stop to watch us in the dark. I couldn't tell who or if it was even a man or a woman, but the idea totally got me off. We had an audience, Honey."

She leaned her body against mine and hugged me.

"Baby, I came!" She said again. She was excited and speaking in hushed tones. "Just from you fucking me. That's never happened before. It was wonderful. You felt so good back there. I felt you everywhere inside me. You reached all the way in and rubbed everything. Oh my God, let's do it again. That's my new favorite position! Your cock felt *huge.*"

I returned her hug and agreed we needed to do it again right away. We moved to the kitchen and grabbed more beer and then found a seat in the living room to talk. I told her about Shelia and Jayne and she got visibly aroused. She has one class with Shelia and has commented many times on how sexy Shelia is. She knows Jayne too and was disappointed she'd missed the action.

It took a minute, but it sank in. I blame her delay on the weed and alcohol.

"Wait," she began. "You were with me. I came back with my beer and told you I was really horny and you took me downstairs. When did you see Shelia and Jayne?"

As if on cue, the other Marc Antony walked through the living room holding Wonder Woman's hand. Jill watched him, her face slowly twisting with understanding. When Marc left the room, Jen looked up at me.

"Oh, fuck. No way."

I held her gaze. She quickly jabbed a hand between her legs and held up glistening sperm-covered fingers. Her mouth moved but no words came out. She stared at her fingers for a bit and then shocked me by laughing. Then she laughed again.

"I do not fucking believe this!" she barked. "You cannot be angry with me. In no way was that cheating."

I said nothing. She rose up and kissed my lips, then got a funny expression.

"Wait. Why didn't you ask me what the hell I was talking about earlier?"

I went blank.

"I tell you I came. I tell you we almost got caught. I even tell you how big you felt and you say nothing? You don't wonder what the fuck I'm talking about? Why? Because you already knew what I had done?"

My mind raced but so did hers. She made the leap.

"Oh my God, that was *you!* You were the person watching us fuck! Why didn't you stop me, Paul? Why did you just watch? What the fuck? You saw some guy fucking me and you let him? This is crazy! How could you do that? Why did you allow him to do that? You saw his costume. You must have realized my mistake. Why did you let another guy fuck me?"

My brain was stuck in neutral.

"Say something!" she demanded, hurt and angry.

A million words swirled in my head but nothing came out. Jen crossed her arms, growing increasingly upset with me.

"Paul!" She stamped her foot.

"It was hot!" I blurted.

Of all the words in my head, those three come out. Great. I braced for the shit-storm. She's petite, but she's a hurricane. As it turned out, I may have accidentally stumbled across the best three words to say. Anything else would have only made things worse. I tripped her up, caught her by surprise. She was stunned. Her mouth fell open. She was speechless!

I ran with it. "I understood immediately," I explained. "He was the only one at fault but I couldn't even blame him; just look at you. I was about to shove him away from you but then you moaned like I've never heard before. I froze. Baby, you looked so sexy, so incredibly erotic. It was like a scene from a movie; unreal and amazing. Everything happened so fast. It seemed like only seconds before you came and then he did. Then I knew you'd be crushed if you saw me standing there. I guess I panicked a little. I'm sorry. I was a little jealous but I was so turned on. You looked like a sex-goddess."

Her anger faded.

"I did?"

"Good God, yes. I was paralyzed. Easily the hottest thing I've ever seen. The situation is so absurd it's like I'm watching a television sit-com. All I saw was your amazing body moving like pure sex. I saw how big he was and what that did to you. Baby I know it's fucked up but I liked it. When he made you orgasm I got hard. I was mesmerized."

She looked down at her body and lifted her breasts to better see her flat stomach. She closed her eyes and I imagined she remembered the feeling of Marc Antony inside her. She shivered. Her nipples stiffened. She opened her eyes.

"Take me back to your place," she ordered and I knew exactly what she thought.

If you guess our sex that night was insane, you're right. Jennifer was aroused by the realization she'd fucked someone new. I ate her pussy without hesitation which sent her into the stratosphere and while I fucked her I made her tell me why she came. She didn't want to but I fucked the truth from her, her words coming to me between grunts and gasps.

"He was so big, Baby" she admitted. "I *had* to cum. His size forced my orgasm. I couldn't hold it back. It was way too soon but I had no choice. His big dick just pushed me off the ledge. I liked that we might get caught too but it was that huge beast stuffed into my pussy that did it. It touched me *everywhere*."

Her words pushed me off the ledge. I

came so hard I saw stars. Because it slows her down and makes her gain weight, Jen uses no birth control. I almost always wear a condom or when we get carried away and fuck without one I'll pull out. Tonight I stayed balls deep. Marc Antony had so why not me too? The realization I added mine to his sent me into the stratosphere. I have no idea why I found that so exciting.

I rested on her for a few minutes but she wanted more and selfishly pushed my head down. I ate her sloppy pussy until she came again. She tasted like him and me and her all mixed and I told her so between licks and that did it for her. What a crazy night.

Strangely, over the next few days jealously *did* make an appearance and eventually sank huge green teeth into my brain. Another guy had fucked my girl. He'd put his bare-naked cock up inside her and she'd *loved* it. I still found the entire experience hot and that only made it more confusing and stressful. I tried talking to her about it a few times but I always chickened out. When she brought it up it was only to laugh about what a crazy night that was. Eventually I reasoned if it didn't bother her why should I let it bother me and filed it away under shit that happens in life. When Jen missed her period my guts twisted into painful knots. The idea that she might carry another man's baby totally fucked with my head although somehow heightened my desire for her and my sexual ferocity when I had her. She commented about what an animal I'd become and how much she loved it but I did not tell her the reason behind my change.

When Jen got her period a week later we both relaxed and our sex-life settled back down to almost normal. The only difference being our frequency increased. No matter how hard I tried, how long or hard I pounded her, what position I tried, I was never able to make her climax using only my penis. Our sex was fantastic and she had no complaints at all, but, still, that truth nagged me. He could do something to her I could not. It bothered me.

Time went by and Christmas break arrived. Sadly, Jen received word that an uncle died and so we made plans to go to California and stay with her parents and attend the funeral. I was a little nervous about meeting her mom and dad although she assured me a thousand times they were really nice people. It took us three days to drive there.

After ten minutes I knew it was true; her parent s were really nice people. They welcomed me into their home like I was part of the family. I expected Jennifer and I would have separate sleeping arrangements but they put us together in her old room. It was fun looking at all her high school awards and trophies. I found her annuals and teased her about being such a nerd, although her annual had way more signatures than mine did.

That night we ate dinner with the family and I met her little sister. Tina had long brown hair and big dark eyes like her older sister, but her skin was so light she looked pale. She wore a huge grey hoodie and giant sweat pants and I couldn't tell if she was fat, skinny, or anywhere in-between. Afterwards we all watched television. Jen surprised me when she said she was tired and ready for bed but I played along. Once she shut and locked her bedroom door, she reached for my belt-buckle.

"What are you doing?" I gasped. "We can't have sex in your parent's house. We are here for a funeral for God's sake."

She laughed. "I know. Besides, my bed squeaks too much. Just let me suck it."

I formed my next argument and I was about to voice it when she sank to her knees and pulled down my zipper. Whatever thoughts I had in my head flew out my dick as her hot mouth closed around it. I fell silent and she chuckled with her mouth full.

The next day she went shopping with her sister and mom and I hung around the house watching football with her dad. After an hour or so I wandered back up to her room to use the Internet. Her dad knocked on the door to let me know he was headed out for a while and minutes later I was alone.

I took a break from the computer and rubbed my eyes. Around the room Jen had a trophy for every way a kid can win a trophy, including ballet and swimming. I wandered around reading every certificate. She also had a thousand photos of her with her friends.

I was about to return to the computer when I noticed an odd slip of paper protruding from the corner of one of her picture frames. I picked it up to push it back in and discovered it was actually a photograph layered behind a photograph. I slipped the back off and withdrew the picture.

The view was down a girl's stomach to her crotch and my lovely girlfriend Jen stared up into the lens, laughing at the same time she licked a pussy. On the back Jen had written, "To the first girl I ever kissed. Love you, Katie."

The picture was printed on standard paper and probably came from the printer sitting in the corner. That told me the picture was probably housed on Jen's computer. Did I want to go snooping?

I studied the picture at length and then put it back. It surprised me but actually was not all that hot; just some girls having fun and figuring things out. I looked out the window at the neighborhood and then turned my attention to her computer.

Yeah, I wanted to snoop.

I went into the program files looking for picture editing software. Once I opened that I clicked on "recent documents" and it took me to a folder she'd labeled "science-project". Clever. I opened it.

I was unprepared.

Dicks. *Lots* of dicks. Some pictures looked like she'd taken them herself and some looked like they'd been sent to her. At the bottom of the page were a series of photographs of Jen sucking one cock after another. She appeared to be the school's blowjob queen.

After I calmed down I began to notice

other details, like in none of them was Jen nude. A few showed her in bra and panties but I got the impression she didn't fuck any of these guys, but she sure helped them keep their balls empty. Many of them showed sperm on her tongue or face. I knew she really enjoyed sex but I never realized how much. My girl was a cock-loving fiend. Many of the penises were featured multiple times so I tried to count how many individual guys and arrived at twenty-five, with a margin of error of three.

I dove back into her computer but found nothing else.

I opened the best pictures of her on the screen and used my phone to snap pictures of my own. In just a few minutes I had a visual record of my girlfriend's cock-sucking history. I became aroused seeing her lips wrapped around all those dicks. I had no idea she was such a slut and now that I knew, I loved it. I bet I could try kinky sex with her and she'd go for it. I'd never fucked a girl in her ass and I got hard as rock thinking I could do it to Jen. I wondered if her computer at her dorm had a similar file of her collegiate conquests and made a note to check if the opportunity ever presented itself.

Her dad came home first but the girls were just minutes behind him. We all had dinner at the table again, which my family never did, and her parents asked me lots of questions. When we got up to her room again for the night I had my dick out in seconds and made her suck it. I manhandled her and when I came I forced my penis deeper into her mouth so she had to swallow it all. I worried I went too far and got carried away but she smacked her lips as her eyes flared with excitement.

"Fuck, Paul, what brought that on? I like it."

I thought about telling her but could not think of how to say it so I said nothing.

"Just horny," I offered.

I went down on her for an hour with visions of oral sex in my head; Jen sucking cock and eating pussy. Every time she started to cum I backed-off, driving her crazy. Finally, I allowed it and she had to cover her face with her pillow.

After she came back to earth she asked, "Holy shit, what has gotten into you? My pussy still tingles, Baby. God! That was amazing."

I felt pretty good about myself.

The funeral was at noon the next day and we all dressed in somber colors. The service was slow and gut-wrenching and Jen cried into my shoulder while Tina cried into hers. Both their dresses billowed at the neck. I had the perfect angle looking down on them and gazed for long minutes at four perfect firm tits. I'm such an asshole. Worse than that, Jen's warm breath on my chest and her arms around me made my dick hard. I prayed it would go away before we had to walk out of the church and it did, but I'm sure both Jen and her sister noticed my bulge. I was mortified.

At the conclusion the pastor said we'd meet again graveside and explained which path to take. Jen asked me to hold back so she could use the restroom. As the others exited, Jen pulled me into an alcove.

"Give it to me," she growled.

"What?"

"Your dick. I know you're hard, you freak. We'll talk later about you getting a hard-on at my uncle's funeral but for now I want to suck it. I need to. Give it to me."

She wasn't actually asking as she yanked open my fly. I kept an eye in every direction. I gasped when her hot mouth closed around me. At the last second I spotted movement by the podium. Tina watched us! Our eyes met.

Jen's suction was intense. There was no romance or affection. Jennifer tried to suck my sperm out, plain and simple. Her hot wet mouth bobbed rapidly on my erection. I was close really fast. She sucked me all the way in and snaked her tongue out to lick my balls and that was it. Boom. Here; have it all. She gagged as she swallowed but tears and red eyes were especially easy to hide today. Tina watched me pump semen down her sister's throat until my eyes closed from pleasure. When I opened them, she was gone.

We joined the others at the grave site and listened to a few more people speak. Her dad held our attention as he described life with his brother. I felt bad for his loss. Tina looked at me with a smirk, but Jen did not notice. Just before I looked away, Tina slipped a finger into her mouth and sucked hard. Brat! From the corner of my eye I saw her fighting laughter.

Dad finished and dropped a rose on the casket. Others stood and followed his action. The coffin began to lower and everyone watched silently. Jen clung to my arm like she feared getting sucking down into the grave too.

The crowd broke up and there was hugging and hushed talking all around. Jen asked if we could give Tina a ride home so her parents could spend time with close friends and of course I said yes.

At home we changed into comfortable clothing. Jen wore a simple green dress but Tina put on fitted white short-shorts and a tight pink top. For the first time I saw her body well and it was pretty fucking amazing. She was athletic like her sister but her boobs were just a little smaller. Her ass was world-class like Jen's. Jennifer was clueless and I realized she only saw Tina as a kid-sister, when she was clearly no longer a kid at all. Tina loved my reaction.

When Jen said she wanted to get out of the house and go for a walk I jumped at the chance. Tina looked disappointed.

I let Jennifer lead the way and we followed a path out of her neighborhood and through a park. I sensed Jen had a lot on her mind so I held her close and talked about inane things like why we have seasons and how old the moon is. As we approached a bench, Jen aimed for it. We sat.

"I need to tell you some things," she began. I nodded. She smoothed the dress on her lap. "I am not the girl you think I am."

I laughed.

"I'm serious, Paul. Don't laugh."

I put on my serious face. She continued.

"I've allowed you to believe I'm this sweet innocent girl, and that's a lie; I'm not. I'm trying to be but I'm not, not really. The more time we spend together the more I like you. After today, how great you were with my family and especially my dad, I really feel myself falling for you. I know the girl is never supposed to say this stuff first but I'm not an ordinary girl."

I took her hands in mine.

"I knew that before I saw all the trophies, Jen, and I'm falling for you too."

She met my eyes, searching.

"I have a past."

"I know," I consoled.

"No, you don't know, and I'm afraid you won't like me once you do know."

"Nothing you could say would drive me away. It doesn't matter what you did before me, only what you do now that we have each other."

She looked hopeful. She wanted to believe I meant it. With sudden insight I realized her past had probably cost her a relationship or two. Most guys would reject her once they knew. Not me. I think it gave her depth and dimension.

"So," she began. "I told you I was a virgin and it's true, I am, or I was until I met you."

I smiled.

"But I have tried stuff. I've done a lot,

actually."

"Just say it, Jen."

"Okay, fuck, here goes; I fooled around with a lot of guys, Paul. A lot."

"But you were a virgin?"

"Yes."

"So, what, like blowjobs and stuff? How many?"

She took a deep breath. "Thirty, maybe thirty-five."

"Wow. Well that explains why you are so amazing at it. Okay, what else?"

She looked at me with disbelief.

"Don't you care?"

"Why would I? Sex is awesome. I love your sex-drive and I know it didn't start the moment you met me. Like I said, it doesn't matter what you did, only what you do. Have you been holding back sexually? Worried you'd scare me away?"

She nodded several times.

"My sweet Baby. You were worried I'd dump you. No way. As far as I'm concerned it only makes you more interesting. Turn it loose, Baby. Set it free. With me, I want you to be the real you."

Tears welled in her eyes. "Paul, that is so incredibly sweet. You're amazing."

"I'm not an ordinary boy," I countered.

She leaned forward and kissed me.

"Remember this moment," she cautioned. "I'm telling you I fucking love sex. *Love* it. I saved my virginity for a special guy but I sure investigated everything else."

"My super-hot girlfriend is telling me she wants more sex? What's not to love? Tell me about it, Jen. Why do you love it so much? What's your favorite thing about it?"

She thought for a minute. "It's complicated. I was scrawny and weird looking until my first year of high school. I love attention and as my body developed I sure got a lot of it. Add gymnastics and guys started staring...men too. Instead of creeping me out I welcomed it. Up there on that balance beam is Heaven. All eyes on me. I'd do it nude if they'd let me. Guys flirted and I flirted right back, hard. Then I met Katie, my best friend in high school. She was wild and already a total slut. I'd never seen a penis so she had her boyfriend show me his and I was hooked. I was fascinated. I had to touch it. Dicks are amazing. Most of my girlfriends thought they looked gross and I guess some are but most are beautiful to me. I was so captivated by his when he spoke again he startled me. I forgot it was attached to him. Sara first showed me how to suck it and then let me try and that was it, I was in love. We sucked his cock together almost every day after school. You should try it, Paul; it's empowering."

I waved her idea away.

She studied my face to see how I took everything so far and continued.

"Katie showed me lots of things. I kissed her and even ate her pussy. I liked it but nothing compares to cock. Baby, I actually *like* the taste of cum. I know that's crazy but it's true. Sometimes I crave it. Only twice have I met a guy that tasted bad. I also love semen for *what* it is. It's a dangerous fluid, like nitroglycerin; handle it carefully or it will blow up in your face and boom, you've made a baby. I've met plenty of guys I didn't like but I've never met a cock I didn't love. I still sucked their dicks even though they were jerks."

My eyebrows went up on that one.

"I warned you," she chastised.

"Does our sex-life satisfy you, Jen?"

"Oh, totally, Paul. No question. I don't need a ton of *different* dicks in my life. It's not like that. One will do. I just need it often. Men like variety. Women, not as much. I feel lucky you're mine, Paul. You're smart and hot and you may not know this but your dick is bigger than average. You're kind and patient and handsome. I'm totally into you."

She smiled. I smiled back, a little bashful.

"So, what I hear you telling me is we will be having a lot more sex."

"If you're interested, Paul, yes, I'd like that."

I was in Heaven. I'm a horny young male. I had been keeping my sex-drive in check so Jen didn't think that's all I wanted her for. Now she told me to ramp it up. God is good.

"Yes, I'd like that too. I even have some ideas I'd like to try."

She shivered.

"I'm yours," she said. "Whatever you want."

I couldn't wait to fuck her firm ass. We stayed another two days. Tina wore one innocently sexy outfit after another and her sister and parents were utterly oblivious. Jen had gone for a run when Tina came out of her bedroom wearing a tiny bikini top and shorts. All her mom said was it looked like she'd out-grown the top and she needed to take her shopping for a new one. Her firm tits were spilling out on every side! Tina watched my face for a reaction and I tried so hard to be indifferent but with her little nipples hardened and poking through the fabric it was too much. I said I had to get some school work done on the computer and excused myself. Jesus. Tina grinned. I left the door to Jen's room open while I surfed and Tina came upstairs twice to get something from her room, parading by me with flirtatious ease. She'd re-tied her top to show more tit. On her last trip up the fabric barely covered her nipples. Jen got back from her run or I think Tina would have shown me her tits.

Jen wanted sex in some form both nights. We couldn't fuck because of the noise but we sure enjoyed each other orally. Now that I knew her secret she showed me what she can do with a penis. I came like a volcano. She really does love the taste of sperm. I used my hands and tongue all over her, finger-fucking her ass while licking her clit. She came harder than ever. I imagine Tina in the next room, ear pressed to wall.

Finally, we were back on the road again. We drove a few hours and then stopped for fuel and Jen changed in the bathroom. When she emerged she wore a white tank-top with no bra and frilly shorts that showed a curve of butt-cheek. She turned heads left and right and now I understood how much she loved it. As soon as we were back in the car I pulled my dick out and she sucked it, neither one of us saying a word. A trucker passed us and blew his horn which made her squirm. She opened her legs, which surprised me, and I know he saw her lace covered pussy. I had a wildcat on my hands and I hadn't even known it.

Our path took us through Vegas and I asked if she wanted to stop.

"Why?" she asked. "I'm not old enough to gamble or drink."

"I am, but I get your point. Maybe we should just drive up The Strip to see all the casinos? I hear it has grown a lot. I've always wanted to see it."

"Okay." She slipped my penis back into her mouth.

We arrived in Vegas with me a few ounces lighter and Jennifer a few ounces heavier. Her tank-top straps barely covered her tits and gusts of wind exposed nipples from time to time. We were safe inside the car but showing off really turned Jen on. After crawling along in traffic for thirty minutes she suggested we get out and walk. I parked the car.

If her exhibitionism in the car turned her on, walking down the street with her tits virtually hanging out drove her wild. I stopped at a liquor store and bought a bottle of Jim Beam Honey and we drank as we strolled. Other girls were dressed like Jen, showing lots of skin and loving the attention. It may have been Fall but it was still really warm.

The sidewalk was packed. We were wedged in with a press of people and there was constant contact with others. Guys would glide by rubbing their shoulders or chest against her nipples, their hands or crotches against her ass. Everyone jostled everyone but it was obvious more males made contact with my girlfriend than with other guys. In fact, all the girls walking seemed to get more than their fair share of contact. The whiskey plus all the attention got Jen worked up and while I wasn't comfortable with them touching her, I knew later I'd benefit.

We stopped at a burger joint and ate and then headed back out. In the bright Vegas sun a hint of darker areola showed through her thin top. Earlier I'd caught her looking down at her own tits so I knew she knew and that turned me on too. We were both ready to fuck in the street and getting hornier by the minute.

Jen suggested we detour and go to the roof of a large parking garage to get a picture down The Strip. I agreed. We cut through some bushes and found an old elevator on the back of a parking structure. It looked mostly unused and Jen gave me a knowing smile. I knew what would happen as soon as those doors closed. At least, what would have happened if this tall Asian guy hadn't joined us at the last second. Once inside he asked me to push the button for the roof. Jen gave me a disappointed look.

One floor from the top, the elevator

stopped. We waited but nothing happened. I pushed a button. I pushed all the buttons. We all looked at each other and Jen asked if now would be a good time to panic. Asian Guy used the elevator phone and we were relieved to hear a comforting female voice on the other end. We were less relieved when she told us this had happened before and help was on the way but it would be a while.

We checked cell phones but the metal and concrete killed reception. We were stuck.

"I'm Paul," I said, extending a hand to our new friend. "And this is Jennifer."

"Hi Paul and Jennifer, I'm Danny."

We all shook hands, Jen's tits jiggling slightly. I passed the bottle to Danny.

We talked until our legs got tired and then we sat and talked some more. He went to UNLV and was supposed to meet friends. He'd just gotten off work and always parked on the roof of this garage and walked across the street. He got stuck in this elevator months before and seemed really calm about it.

We told him our funeral story and he told Jen he was sorry for her loss. Mostly we just swapped college stories about finals and professors. Every now and then, when he thought he could get away with it, he ran his eyes all over Jen. He was sly but I knew to watch for it. The cold metal elevator made her nipples stiffen and she was killing Danny and me. She looked so sexy in her shorts and top my penis grew. When I noticed she looked directly at my crotch, I got flustered.

She chuckled. "I feel the same way,"

she teased.

Jen turned the conversation towards college parties and asked if Danny had any wild stories. He talked about the difficulty of attending a university in the heart of Sin City and all the infinite distractions. Jen asked him what he found most distracting and he answered instantly; "hot women." We all laughed. By now the bottle was almost empty.

I said, "I don't have that distraction. I already have the hottest woman on the planet."

Danny quickly agreed. Partly I bragged to another male collegian and partly I genuinely meant it, but Jill lit up. She crawled over to me on all fours and planted a hot, wet, sensuous kiss on my lips. I returned it, long enough to feel embarrassed in front of Dan.

When I opened my eyes to check on him, I discovered Jen's top hung away from her body and her glorious naked tits were on full display. Danny's eyes were glued to them. Jen had to know she showed them to everybody and just didn't care. She kept her eyes closed and continued the kiss and when her tongue parted my lips and crept into my mouth, I played with it using my tongue.

I felt her hand on my zipper and started to look down but she only kissed me more urgently. I felt cool air on my penis and then she swooped and her hot mouth engulfed my dick. Fuck it felt good. I took four full seconds to remember Danny was right there. I looked at him but he was enthralled watching pretty Jen suck dick. Every girl looks cuter with a hard penis in her mouth.

Dan rubbed the front of his pants. I put both hands on Jen's head and pushed my dick farther into her mouth. She moaned and sucked harder.

"Holy shit, Jennifer," Danny exclaimed, "You're fucking amazing."

She did not look at him but stopped sucking long enough to pull her top off. She held my balls up and licked them before putting my shaft back in her mouth. I was nervous Danny would try something but he seemed to understand look but don't touch. He pulled his dick out and jacked while watching Jen work. He wasn't as big as me.

Jen saw movement and twisted her head to see Danny. When she realized he jacked-off watching her she groaned and reached inside her shorts to play with her pussy. I was surprised when she came first. Danny was next with thick bolts of pure white jizz landing right by Jen. I came just as Danny finished, lifting my hips and filling my girl's mouth with a huge load.

I fell back against the cold steel wall and Jen hugged my chest. Danny was still on his knees, soft dick almost touching the floor, staring at Jen and her perfect tits. After a while he laughed and then so did we.

Jen offered us the last of the whiskey but we refused. "Good," she teased. "Need to rinse my mouth out anyway."

I put my dick away and so did Daniel but Jen left her top off, acting like it was no big deal. Conversation started up again but we avoided talking about what just happened.

An hour later maintenance guys called and said they were on site and would have us down soon. Jen dressed. When we felt the elevator move we cheered.

They meet us on the roof and we shook hands with them and Danny, who jumped in his cars to meet his friends. Jen snapped a tons of pictures. We took the stairs down.

By the time we got back to the car it was too late to get back on the road. We found a cheap motel room downtown and showered. The room had hardcore porn and Jen wanted to watch it so we did. After three hours she'd seen enough and, wildly horny, wanted to get out of the room. We put on fresh clothing and hit the street. I wore jeans and a T-shirt and sandals, Jennifer wore a denim skirt and long-sleeve tight white top. She debated over a bra but then decided against. She went with sandals too.

Downtown Vegas is nothing like The Strip. Creepy guys and prostitutes hung out at every alley. People shuffled along without looking up seemingly without hope. Jen moved a little closer to me. Fremont Street was well lit but the various alley and roads leading off of it were not. We stopped at an intersection and a flashing neon sign caught her eye; *Nude girls! Nude guys! Hot sex show!*

She looked up at me and grinned. I grinned back. We turned down the alley and approached the doorman.

"Over eighteen?" he barked.

"I am," Jennifer insisted.

He held out a hand wearing a red leather glove with the fingers missing. "Card."

Jen pulled her driver's license from her small purse and handed it to him. He looked back and forth from it to her face and leered. "Welcome," he said. He opened the deep red door behind him and ushered us in. I guess I look older than eighteen.

A jet-black hallway led away from the door. We had some light as long as the door to the street remained open but as soon as he closed it behind us we were in pitch-blackness. Jen grabbed my arm and I felt our way forward. The hallway made a sharp right and we walked into a heavy black drape. I found the split and opened it. A bored girl wearing a glowing bikini stood at a podium with another heavy curtain behind her.

"Twenty bucks," she drawled.

I reached for my wallet.

"Each."

I handed her forty dollars and she pulled back the second drape.

We stepped into a small dark theater. On the far wall was a half-circle stage under deep blue lights. About twenty folding chairs curled around the stage and more than half were occupied, almost all men. Jen and I stopped to watch the stage.

A queen-sized bed stood there, missing head and foot board, the mattress covered by a dark fitted sheet. In the center of the bed a girl rested on all fours, straddling a man, his thick and shiny penis sliding repeatedly up into her. I heard Jen gasp. Behind the girl another worked his hard cock in and out of her ass. At her face, a third man held her head and slow-fucked her mouth, pushing a long cock several inches down her throat. She looked drugged and bewildered but reacted to the sensations as each cock penetrated her. Behind the girl and along the back of the stage, four more men, slowly stroking penises in various stages of arousal, waited their turn with her. All the air left Jennifer's lungs and she fumbled to hold my hand.

"Baby, that's sooooo hot," she whispered.

I took a step forward to find a seat but Jen pulled me back. She wanted to stay back here in the dark, far from the stage and the other patrons. I put my back against the wall and held her in front of me.

The men had no interest in pleasing the woman, although she clearly felt a great deal of pleasure. They fucked her holes however they saw fit. When the man in her ass ejaculated deep in her bowels, he withdrew his cock and another man took his place. She arched her back as he penetrated her but the penis in her mouth smothered any cry of pleasure or pain.

Jen and I watched in silence. The girl began to grind her hips on the man beneath her and shortly we heard her muffled cries of orgasm. The man in her mouth emptied his balls down her throat and wandered away, replaced by the man next in line.

"I'm going to fuck your ass," I

whispered hotly. "Just like that girl up there."
She pressed her body more firmly against
mine.

One by one each man used the girl on
the bed. She used them back but the fight
was not fair. She did have another orgasm
and a strong one but mostly she was just
there for the men to enjoy. One by one they
came inside her and left.

When the last man shot her full, he left
the stage and she fell to the bed, exhausted.
A girl walked onto the stage announcing the
next show would take place in thirty minutes.
I nudged Jen towards the door but her eyes
were glued to the girl on the bed. Eventually
everyone left but us and the girl.

Jen approached the bed.

The girl heard us coming and raised
up on one elbow. No doubt she expected
some man who wanted to fuck her so when
she saw Jen her face lit up as much as the
drugs would allow.

"You're really pretty," she said to Jen,
reaching out for her. Jen took her hand.

"What's your name?" Jennifer asked.

"Sara. What's yours?"

"Jennifer. Jen."

The girl rose to her knees. She had
dark hair pinned up, although the deep blue
lights made it impossible to tell what color
exactly. As soon as Jen got close enough
Sara rose up and held her face and kissed
my girlfriend deeply. Jen, caught by surprise,
hesitated for half a second and then returned
the kiss. When they broke for air my girl
licked her lips and I realized she tasted the

semen of the man that just emptied his balls in Sara's mouth. My girl looked over her shoulder at me.

"Is this okay, Paul?"

What guy is threatened by another girl? I told Jen it was no problem and they went back to kissing. I heard a door close behind the stage wall and then footsteps. A pretty girl stepped from backstage and tossed an envelope of money on the bed. Sara picked it up. That was when I noticed her wedding ring.

"You're married?" I asked.

"Yes. Surprised? My husband was one of the men in the audience."

"You're a lucky girl," Jen stated. They kissed deeply again.

"I could kiss you all night," she told Jen. "You're a natural beauty. My husband would devour you. If your man said it was alright, of course. I'm here again Saturday night if you're still in town."

They kissed a little more and Sara slipped away and trotted off stage.

"What a crazy place," Jen breathed.

"What a crazy town," I countered. "After school we should consider moving here."

Jen gave me a funny look and took my hand.

"That's a good plan," she said.

"Do you want to stay for the next show?" I asked.

Jen looked around the theater. "Just to see what it is, okay?"

I reclaimed my spot against the wall

and wrapped my arms around Jen. Men began to enter and take seats. The blue spotlights turned into one deep red over the bed. Two guys appeared and wheeled the bed off-stage and then two more appeared and wheeled a new bed to take its place. On this bed a young girl was tied face-up, ankle and wrist. She was blindfolded and gagged. The girl struggled convincingly against her bonds.

"Uh oh," Jen muttered. "Is this real or an act?"

From backstage a masked man appeared sporting the largest erection I'd ever seen. I quickly glanced down at Jen for her reaction and even in the dark saw her wide desire-filled eyes and open mouth.

"Jesus," she breathed.

The man approached the bed and touched the girl and she jumped and kicked. He ran a hand up her leg and she tried to throw him off but her manacles prevented her. He moved up the bed until his erection loomed over her writhing, struggling body. Jen couldn't look away but neither could I. He lowered his hips and we heard the girl cry out as his massive cock began to penetrate her.

"Get me out of here, Paul" Jen exhaled.

The exit sign was across the room and I led us towards it. We passed through two more drapes and followed a twisting hallway and the last door dumped us on the street. Jen walked fast, putting distance between that place and herself. After we walked a few blocks she stopped.

"That was intense," she said.

"It was."

"Do you think she was only acting?"

I played taped in my head. "Yeah. Too many people involved. Plus, all those backstage. Someone would go to jail."

Jen shivered. "His dick was big."

"I'm guessing you liked that part."

She laughed. "Was it that obvious?"

Three prostitutes walked by and looked us up and down but decided we weren't worth their time. I saw Jen study them. After a minute to catch our breath Jen took off again. We'd gone another three or four blocks when Jen looked back over her shoulder.

"Can you imagine living like that?"

"The theater?"

"The prostitutes. Paid for sex. That part sounds good but you'd have to fuck whoever wanted you. I'm not sure I'd like that part."

I laughed. "You're not sure?"

She laughed too. "Yeah, good point. Obviously I'm assuming I would not be in a relationship with you. I imagine you'd have a hard time allowing me to fuck other guys for a living."

"Absolutely."

Suddenly Halloween night flashed in my mind. I saw Jen shoved up against a stack of boxes and Marc Antony fucking her from behind. I heard her muffled cries of pleasure as his fat cock ripped an orgasm from her. I shook my head.

Jen continued. "Honestly, I'm totally

fine with the sex for money part. I have no moral qualms. I can buy you dinner or give you the money to buy your own dinner. I just want the option of declining a motherfucker if he gives me the creeps."

I got the impression this was not the first time she'd considered this lucrative career. There were girls back on campus that moonlighted as escorts to pay for college. I wondered if Jen knew any of them. Then something occurred to me. Had she already tried it before I met her? Her parents had money; not a ton, but enough she wouldn't *need* to do it. I filed my questions away for later.

We walked the mile or so to the end of the street and did a huge loop back up the other side. Guys leered at Jen almost every step of the way but where it made me nervous earlier, I found myself enjoying it now. They wanted her but she was mine. I felt proud to have a girl this hot with me. She clearly could pick any man she wanted and he'd jump at the chance but here she hung on my arm.

I stopped at another liquor store and bought a fresh bottle of whiskey for back at the room. Jen was only out of my sight for ten minutes. When I left the store and stepped back out onto the sidewalk she had three tall black guys around her.

As soon as she saw me she ended her conversation with them and slipped out of their circle. She took my hand and we headed back to the room.

"What did they want?" I asked.

"Blowjobs, probably. They asked my name and where I was from and why I was all alone on Fremont Street."

"Were you scared?"

"No. Actually, it was kind of exciting."

"Some night we've had."

"Like, amazing. Vegas drips sex. It's saturated with it. We definitely have to come back here again."

We did not know it at the time, but years later we would.

We returned to our motel and ordered more porn. Jen was especially horny and before I could try to conquer her ass, she told me to fuck it. She sucked my dick to get it wet and then sat her sphincter down on top of me. I pushed up into her hot ass and she fucked me hard, rubbing her clit and playing with her tits. She came like bomb. We cleaned up, slept, fucked again, slept, fucked again, and then finally slept until morning.

We returned to school and time flew by. Classes came and went, finals came and went, weeks became months and months became a year. We both earned good grades, concentrating more on our studies than the frequent parties around us. I became a junior and Jen became a sophomore. We both took jobs over the summer and prepared for next year.

With one exception, we shared our amazing sex-life with no one.

Towards the end of summer, a friend threw a house party and invited everyone still in town. Word spread and by the time the party rolled around the crowd was massive. I was supposed to meet her before so we would attend together but coach was pissed so I got stuck at baseball practice. We agreed I'd just meet her at the party.

She texts me later the party was rocking and loud so she was putting her phone in her purse and would check it later. By the time I got to the party she'd been there well over an hour without me.

I finally found her in back at the pool. The guys had set-up a small trampoline on the deck and everyone bounced off it into the deep end. It all may have started innocently but the party was now almost two hours old and everyone was at least buzzed and many outright drunk. A football player went off the trampoline and at the height of his arc, pulled his shorts down and flashed the crowd everything before hitting the water. The idea instantly took hold and the next person, an Asian girl, ripped her top off as she reaches her zenith. From that moment every person jumping removed an article of clothing. Within minutes it was a totally nude sporting event.

Jennifer jumped a minute later and performed a split at the top of her arch. When she spread her legs her little bald pussy opened up like a blossom. Her gorgeous tits and fresh pink slit were displayed for all to see. The crowd went crazy, the girls as wild as the guys. The next girl up did the same thing. The next guy swept a girl into his arms and kissed her as they jumped together.

I saw Jen talk to some huge jock next to her and he nodded. She climbed on him piggy-back, her hot little pussy pressed right against his spine, her strong legs wrapped around his waist, her tone arms wrapped around his neck. He moved towards the trampoline like Jen's weight meant nothing. He had a large penis and it flopped and bounced as he carried her. He jumped and she held on and they hit the water like a bomb, splashing everyone.

Besides the nudity, which is not automatically sexual, there was nothing carnal or erotic about what everyone was doing. This was pure college hijinks. Sexy, yes, but not necessarily sexual. Not yet. Not until Jen and her new friend took a second leap off the spring-board and this time she held on facing him.

Because they were wet she slid down his body until her pussy rested on the base of his dick. He had trouble walking because her firm butt blocked his thighs so he had to waddle to the trampoline. His cock thrummed across her labia. As they struggled for a more effective grip, her slit rode up and down his veiny shaft. The crowd went just a little quieter at what they were witnessing. I went rock hard.

I could not tell you why to save my life. As if everyone we went to school with seeing her nude wasn't bad enough, now here she crawled all over another guy. I know she'd swear it was all innocent fun, and maybe she was right, but it got to me and got to me in surprising ways. She was obviously drunk, as were they all, and the best time to act young and stupid is when you are young and stupid, so I still had no real reason to get angry. I took a deep breath. I trembled. Part of me was embarrassed. Part of me was hurt. Part of me was jealous. All that made sense. But part of me, as my erection attested, was clearly powerfully aroused, and that made no logical sense.

Football Guy wrapped his arms around her torso and pulled her close. Her tits mashed his chest. Her asshole and pussy were spread for all to see. He cupped her ass and bounced and they hit the water hard, laughing.

Couples jumped together now; holding hands, hugging, kissing. Threesomes joined in. The water in the pool sloshed and splashed. Groups held hands and jumped together.

I scanned the crowd, amazed at all the hot pussy and firm titties. Like Jen, most girls were hairless. A few had pubic hair but not many. The crowd was in good shape, like only the male and female athletes felt comfortable playing this particular game. Lots of other students, like me, stood back and watched.

Her new friend grabbed a buddy and they sandwiched Jen between them and jumped again. She had muscles and penises pressed against her front and back and Football Guy started to swell, as did the guy behind her. Some couples had moved to the side to make out.

Jen was absolutely comfortable nude. Not a shred of self-consciousness perturbed her. I ran my eyes up and down her like I saw her naked for the first time and realized her reaction made perfect sense. She should be proud naked. Judging by the long stares she received from both sexes, they felt the same way I did.

Eventually I left my spot and worked my way around the pool. I grabbed a towel and wormed through the crowd and when Jen saw me she clapped with joy and ran to give me a hug. Someone in the crowd snatched the towel away and so I just hugged her soaking wet body to my dry one.

Jen took my hand and went searching for her clothing. After a short time, she stood before me in shorts and bikini top. We headed for the open bar while the pool party raged and Jen never looked back for Football Guy. Nothing she did gave me any reason to doubt her loyalty and everything she did gave me reason to trust her. We grabbed two beers and found a quiet place to talk. She cut right to it.

"Did that bother you? Out by the pool? Did I go too far, Baby?"

"No. Maybe a little, but nothing to worry about. You were having fun."

I realized she was a little more drunk than I'd assumed. She'd tied her top loosely and the little triangles of fabric barely covered her firm tits.

"Did you like it?"

I thought about lying but rejected the idea instantly.

"You know; I have to admit I did a little. I love watching you have fun. You love to show off and you're so sexy when you do. Not to mention you look amazing, Baby. You have an incredible body."

"You like other people's eyes on me?"

"I do. I don't know if I like it for me or if I like it for you, if you know what I mean."

"I think I do." She took a step closer to me. "I think you like it for you *and* you like it for me, but mostly you like it for you."

"Why do you say that?"

She rose on her toes so her face was close to mine and lowered her voice.

"You watched another man fuck me and did nothing to stop him."

A fire lit in my gut. Why bring that up now? Where was she going with this?

"That was an accident," I countered. "You thought it was me. I couldn't get angry with you. In your mind you were having sex with me."

"Not me, Baby, *him.* You were so fair about it, so logical. What man does that? Why didn't you run up and shove him away from me the second you saw what was happening? That reaction should have been instinctive and automatic. Instead you *watched.*"

She moved closer, pressing her warm body against mine. "Tell me the truth, Paul; did it turn you on to see me getting fucked? Hm? Did you enjoy that huge cock moving in and out of me? Did my moans turn you on? I bet you loved it when he made me cum."

Her voice was slow and slightly slurred. She'd had a lot of booze and I reasoned that's what made her so aggressive. She kissed me hard, forcing her tongue into my mouth.

"I saw you watching me at the pool," she said. "You have almost as much fun as I do when I act like a slut. Those guys had their hands all over me, their bodies pressed right up against mine. I felt their cocks all over my ass and legs."

My penis began to grow and Jen felt it.

"Ha! I knew it! Aw, Baby, you loooooove your little slut girlfriend?"

Circuits snapped shut in my brain faster than I could track them. I raced towards a logical conclusion with blinding speed. One emotional deduction led to the next and before I could stop it, an absolute truth left my mouth.

"Yes, Jen, I do love you. I do. I love you."

She eased back on her heels, face frozen. Neither of us dared move. Water slowly filled her eyes. A smile spread, threatening to reach both ears. I was suddenly vulnerable and exposed and terribly frightened.

"Say it again," she breathed.

I did not hesitate. "I love you, Jen."

She squealed and threw her arms around my neck, kissing me wildly.

"I love you too! I love you too! I love you too!" she said, mashing her lips to my face each time. "I've loved you before the funeral, but that sealed it. You're perfect for me, Paul. I'm so happy to hear you say it!"

Maybe not the ideal setting to announce one's true heart but isn't life always messy? Relief flooded my chest and I felt my insides relax. I'd been holding back those feelings for months without realizing it and now that I'd voiced them, and heard her return my love, my joy was complete. I returned her hot and passionate kisses. We left the party and headed to my place and only stopped making love once we were both exhausted.

Jen moved in. I've heard that's sometimes the beginning of the end, but not for us. We have the same ideals about being a respectful roommate and treated each other well. We continued to prioritize school with only the occasional party here and there. Her friends approved of me and mine of her, although most of mine could not take their eyes off her whenever she was around.

We talked a few times about her behavior at the pool party and my reaction to it. The truth was I did enjoy each and every time she acted slutty. I'd roll with it when it was her idea but I was not comfortable suggesting it. It had to come from her and then I just held on for the ride. She went months with nothing that approached the debauchery of that pool party, but she did stop wearing a bra and often skipped panties too. She touched no one but she sure drove some boys crazy, which drove her crazy, which drove me crazy. She'd come home and fuck my brains out. She rarely flirted with another guy in front of me. He had to be something special for her to do that.

Finals rolled around again and I became a senior and Jen became a junior.

We took a few summer-school courses to get ahead and one day we were in the library studying when Jen got my attention.

I looked up at her.

"Look over there," she said with a jerk of her chin.

A muscular guy sat in a large reading chair by the window. He wore shorts and a T-shirt and his gaze bounced back and forth between two large medical books.

"Recognize him?" she asked.

I looked again, scanning.

"No."

She closed her book. Today she wore a short tennis skirt and tight white tank-top and, at the moment, a sly grin. She stood and walked a long circle around Muscles and took a chair opposite him. She got comfortable, as if she were reading, and settled into the big chair. Minutes passed but eventually Muscles looked up and when he did his eyes landed right on her crotch. I had both their profiles so I had no idea what he saw but based on his reaction I'd say a pretty panty-covered pussy looked back at him.

I played it cool and when Muscles looked around I had my head buried in my book. Jen innocently allowed her legs to part and she sure had his attention now. She rocked one leg back and forth and his eyes were glued to her lap. Soon he had to adjust how he sat and I knew why.

Jen continued to act nonchalant, like the book she read fascinated her, and I enjoyed her teasing this guy. He grew more uncomfortable by the minute but couldn't look away. At least his eyes now roved her entire body, lingering on her pretty face. Jen moved her other leg and I knew his view must be spectacular.

Then I noticed his cock inching down the leg of his shorts. The large head and an inch of shaft rested on the seat of his chair and it looked like there was more behind that. I switched to watch Jen's face and when she saw it her coy smile faded. Two more inches eased out. This guy was big. Really big.

Then I realized who this was.

Marc Antony, from the Halloween party almost two years ago. Not only had that big dick been inside Jen, it had made her orgasm like she never had before or since and then filled her with sperm. That cock right there, no more than fifteen feet away. That cock slowly creeping towards the edge of the cushion.

Jen had somehow recognized him and immediately wanted to tease him. How had she known? More importantly, why did she want to flirt with him of all people? Especially with me sitting right here watching her.

Jen's eyes were riveted to his cock just like his eyes were riveted to her pussy. The air around us became electrified with sexual tension. Outwardly all of us still acted ignorant of each other but internally we were seething with lust. I know Jen only planned on flirting with him but she was rapidly falling under his spell.

He casually adjusted his position again, innocently tugging his shorts to the side, but what he really did was create more space to expose his cock. The library was virtually deserted during summer school so no one was around. As his penis filled with blood it lifted off the seat, the head bounced slightly in time with his heart beat. Jen rolled both lips into her mouth and bit down on them.

I turned a page of my book as if I were reading and both of them shot a glance at me. Satisfied I was unaware of his actions, Marc Antony turned his attention back to her.

Jen opened her legs wider. At last I saw her pussy and I was surprised to discover she wore no panties. I should have known. She'd probably planned to fuck me after her workout but then all this had happened. Marc gazed directly at my girlfriend's small hairless slit. This flirting just got a whole lot more serious. With the pink, delicate, inner-folds of her pussy displayed like this, Jen seemed to be inviting him into her body.

My penis twitched. Jen had gone from teasing flirt to lusty slut but for some reason I really liked it. She had this dude hypnotized. He was dying to fuck her and didn't even realize he already had. On the other hand, Jen *did* know and that made her escalate this from flirting to borderline fore-play. I felt feverish.

Marc Antony's cock was now only held down by the leg of his shorts. He was big and hard and throbbing and red. Jen drooled. She remembered that cock well.

Voices drifted to us from around the corner and both of them closed their legs. A group of freshmen wandered by, bewildered by the size of the place, and headed up the stairs to Reference. I watched them all the way.

When I looked back, Marc had taken the bold step of pulling his cock out the leg of his shorts. That thick and vein-covered pillar of flesh stood up from his lap like a cannon. Jen met his eyes and then dropped her gaze to his cock and he slowly wrapped his fingers around it and tugged. She furrowed her brow with lusty want. Her eyes flicked to me and then back to him and I took that moment to slip out of my chair and behind a bookcase. She could see me but he could not. She wasn't looking at me but she could see me if she chose to. She didn't.

She was now as hypnotized as he. Her hand slid down and found her clit and she rubbed in time with him. Her face began to flush and it spread to her throat and chest. Their absolute silence was erotic. She came quickly, slamming her knees closed on her hand and arching her neck. Her legs shook.

Too bad for him more voices approached and he quickly tucked his erection away. I returned to my seat with a random book from the shelf and he spotted me for the first time. *Sorry, dude, show's over,* I thought. Jen looked up and acted like she saw me for the first time and joined me at my table. I played along; *hey, hi, how are you? Good. What grade did you get in organic chemistry?*

He did not hang around. Frustrated, he packed up his books into his backpack and slung it over a shoulder. As he walked by

I impulsively spoke to him. I thought it would be fun to watch Jen's reaction.

"Hey, aren't you Brian Delessy?" I asked. "We had a glass together freshman year?"

He stopped. He answered me but his eyes were welded to Jen. "No, my name is Mark Anthony. I'm the starting quarterback for the Badgers."

Ha! Holy shit! No wonder he'd worn that costume! His name was so close!

"Oh, sorry, my mistake. I don't follow football."

"You got a build on you though. Baseball? Lacrosse?" He turned back to Jen. "You, too. Gymnastics? Swimming? Tennis?"

"All of the above," she replied with a sweet smile.

"How do the Badger's chances look this year?" I asked.

"Great."

I invited him to have a seat and he jumped at it. To keep things from feeling too weird, I intentionally left girlfriend out and introduced Jen as my friend and study-buddy. I acted oblivious to the shenanigans they'd just shared. Jen went along with me.

The three of us talked about school and sports and classes for almost an hour. Jen only listened to him with one ear; her eyes were too busy memorizing every square inch of his stud-frame. I enjoyed my little game and Jen did too. Their tension was palpable. As our time with him grew, so did the look in her eyes. Jennifer wanted him so badly. His desire rose too. He said and did everything exactly right to push her buttons. Sexually, he was perfect for her. My sweet Jennifer wanted this man more than any man before him, including me.

He mentioned an upcoming party and we quickly swapped numbers.

Soon enough Mark had to leave for class and once he was gone Jen jumped over and hugged me fiercely.

"Oh my fucking God!" Jen yelped. "You are amazing. So smooth, Baby. He had no idea."

"How about that name?" I said, laughing.

"Baby, you are so cool. I knew you would figure out who that was but you played it beautifully. I'm so impressed. Weren't you jealous? I wanted to tease both of you but you are the king. You flipped my game back on me. You win."

"Thank you, thank you." I bowed to the non-existent audience. "I have to ask, Jen, how did you know it was the guy from Halloween? We all wore masks that night and the room was so dark. How did you figure out he was the guy?"

"I already knew who he was. I knew two days after the party. My girlfriend Stacey was down in the game room that night, making out with some dude on one of the couches. She recognized me when I walked by with him and knew him from his body because she'd fucked him a few weeks earlier. Her suspicion was confirmed by the small tattoo on his hand. She was surprised to see me with him because she knew I was crazy about you but figured what the hell, to each their own. She asked me about it days later and I told her what happened. She took my hand and walked me to the cafeteria and pointed out whom I had actually fucked. She got a good laugh about that."

"Why didn't you tell me all this?"

"And hurt your feelings? Why? As long as he was some anonymous guy he was no threat. I imagined telling you it was the Badgers starting quarterback that fucked me and you'd be crushed. What if you had classes with him? What if you two were friends already? I couldn't imagine telling you a friend of yours had fucked me. I saw no good purpose to telling you so I didn't."

Valid points.

"What about Stacey? Does she know I know?"

"That Mark fucked me? Yes. When I told her your reaction she punched my shoulder, called me a bitch, and said she wanted to be me. She thinks you're hot and it is totally unfair that I got to fuck Mark and then come home to you. Of course I rub it in every chance I get."

I remembered Stacey and smiled. I thought she was hot too. I was mildly disturbed one of her friends knew the truth but also found it strangely arousing.

"You took that teasing thing pretty far." I said.

She looked embarrassed. "Way farther than I intended, that's for sure. I just wanted to get you both worked up a little and then leave you twisting. Isn't his dick gorgeous? Is it okay if I say that? He's handsome and his body is awesome but that dick gives me goose bumps. Does it bother you when I say shit like that, Baby?"

"No, Jen, I always want to know what you're thinking."

It did bother me but I felt immature saying so. I knew in a few minutes my irritation would be over so why mention it?

We went back to reading for a time and then headed for home. I desperately wanted to leave my penis buried inside her when I came but pulled out at the last second. My orgasm rocked me. I started talking to her as I ate her and when I asked if she still thought about Mark's big cock she cried yes and came hard and sent pussy-juice gushing into my mouth.

I gave her a few minutes to come down and then sent my tongue softly curling around her engorged clit. Her nerves were on fire so I stayed right below the threshold of too much and soon had her writhing on our bed climbing the hill to another orgasm.

I tried to think of a way to make things even more exciting but no ideas came to me. I wracked my brain searching for something sexy and daring yet flirty and fun. I kept her climax just out of reach as tried to think of something to make her explode. I knew she fantasized about Mark and I didn't blame her. In fact, I felt perfectly secure in our relationship. I felt like Jen and I were in on the joke and Mark was the outsider. I got an idea.

I slowed my tongue down and slipped

two fingers inside her drenched pussy.

"I think I'm going to nurture my friendship with Mark," I began. "He's a cool guy, right? I bet he knows everybody, gets invited to all the parties. I can dangle you as bait, make him think he has a chance to fuck you."

Jen sucked air and held it. Her body had grown taut so I knew my words were affecting her. This was fun.

"Did you see how he looks at you?"

Jen moaned. She *wanted* Mark to look at her like that. She'd seen the look in his eye and longed to believe it was real and I'd just confirmed it. I licked faster. Mark could have any girl on campus and Mark wanted Jen. Jen ate it up. Jen felt special.

I wiggled my tongue far up inside her pussy and sucked on her labia. I withdrew it and pushed a thumb in to rub her G-spot while I feather-whipped her swollen clit. I remembered Mark standing behind my girl.

"Halloween is three months away. If we all wear masks I might let him fuck you again. I'm sure you'd love that. Can you feel his big cock, Baby? Can you remember him inside?"

BOOM. Jen's body went as rigid as steel. Her heels dug in and her toes curled and her mouth opened in a silent scream. Her fists gripped the comforter and her pussy convulsed, squeezing the blood out of my thumb. I remembered his massive erection driving in and out of her and felt sure her pussy had gripped him the way it now gripped me.

"OOOOoooohhhhhhhh ffffuuuuuuuuuuck!" she screamed.

I whipped her clit even faster and pumped my thumb and a second spike smashed into her. Her head thrashed side to side.

"Mark! Oh, Baby, Fuuuuuuck Meeeeee!"

I grazed her clitoris with my bumpy tongue and rocked her entire body with a third spike of pleasure, more powerful than the previous two. I remembered his death-grip on her hips as he emptied his load inside her.

Her pussy squirt into my mouth and spasms wracked her tight cunt. She no longer formed words; only loud animal grunts and groans poured out of her. I'd wanted to make her cum hard and I'd succeeded. I'd also discovered how badly she wanted him.

I'd guess her climax lasted almost a minute. Once it drained away she sank deep into the bed, exhausted. She lay absolutely still. I stared down at her perfect face and perfect body and slipped out of the bedroom.

An idea had formed and I needed to contemplate without the incredible distraction of a nude Jen; could I *actually* allow Mark to fuck her again? I'd said it to drive her over the edge but hearing the words created an image and it was an image I found exciting. That he wanted it was a given. That she wanted it was almost as certain. That I wanted it was a very good possibility but that was crazy. What man would want such a thing?

But I think I did.

I closed my eyes and heard Jen call out Mark's name as she came. I knew what he would do to her. My sweet Jennifer would surrender her body to him. She would offer him everything. I knew there was an excellent chance, almost a guarantee, that he would please her more than I ever had, that sex with him would be more exciting for her than sex with me. That worried me. If I granted her this, she'd hold nothing back. She'd set free her inner-slut without reservation. There was no question about Jen's love for me. Hot Mark would be for sex and Jen would embrace their mating fully and completely, knowing when it was over she would return to me; a loving, nurturing, and supportive relationship. It would be a slut dream arrangement.

Don't women hold something back when they make love? Men can't be trusted. Women learn early that if you give a man everything he'll take it and then fuck someone else too. Better to keep your guard up, never let him fully into your heart, string him along.

That's a decent strategy and Jen has probably used it on men she met before me, but we are beyond that now. Our hearts have melted together and reformed as one. She would not play that game with Mark. She'd let her guard down. She'd lose herself with him knowing I waited for her.

I couldn't do it. As exciting as the idea was, I couldn't hand my girl over to him. I knew in my gut what he'd do to her, what he'd make her feel. I knew he'd take her to heights I'd never reach and the rest of my time with her I'd always wonder how much she craved it, no matter what she told me. I'd seen the way she looked at him. I'd seen the way he looked at her. These two were an atomic bomb waiting to detonate.

The rest of my time with her. I imagined my life with Jen and tried to picture a time when I might not be with her. We'd been together for three years and an official couple for just over one. Before too long I'd graduate and she'd remain in school. Would our relationship end? Would we stay together? Could we survive that? The thought of losing her crushed my heart. I couldn't bear it. I could not allow it.

I went to the hall closet. Careful to let her sleep, I began searching the boxes I had in storage. Four crates later, I found it. I pulled the little black box out and dusted it off. I opened the small lid and my mother's wedding ring gleamed. My father had given it to me after my mom's passing. At the time I couldn't imagine I'd use it but my father had insisted. He was always wiser than me.

I held it up to the dim light and the diamonds and emeralds glittered in whites and greens. I put it back into the tiny box and held it tight. I repacked the closet.

I said nothing to Jen about Mark. I tried to put it behind us but it ate at me. She was all class and made no mention of him but I knew he bounced around inside her brain.

After a week the urge to watch Jen misbehave grew too strong and I suggested we study at the library again. It was the same day and time we'd encountered Mark the first time.

As expected, Mark was back at the same chair. We are all such creatures of habit. He was surrounded by four friends, other football players by the look of them, with him at the head of the table.

Jen caught on instantly and flashed me a knowing smile. I wanted to watch her get worked up but without the risk of anything happening, so I figured another library show was best. This was probably the safest venue. We'd have a fun and flirtatious afternoon and then run home and fuck like animals again.

He looked up and a huge smile split his face. I shook his hand but Jen gave him a big hug. Her hot little body looked so sexy up against his big muscular one. We pulled chairs up to his and joined their group. Again, the library was virtually empty.

After five minutes of conversation, with every guy at the table trying to impress Jen, she announced she needed to visit the little girls room. As soon as she was gone all five guys were on me; are you her boyfriend? Is she single? Is she a model? Have you seen her naked? Does she have a website? Do you think she'd go out with me? I informed them no, I wasn't her boyfriend, just a good friend, and you all can ask her about anything else you want to know. Mark looked at me and asked again if I was her boyfriend or if I had feelings for her because it seemed to him I did.

"What man can look at her and not want her?" I responded. "But she doesn't see me in that way. Too bad. Best of luck to you all."

They all started talking at once. Mark silenced them.

"I love you bros," he stated. "But pack it up and get the fuck out of here. She's mine."

They all gave him a ton of shit but they all packed up their books and laptops and headed out. Mark was the boss.

Jen returned and Mark explained the guys had to leave for practice and she bought it. We'd been talking about forty-five minutes and Jen told a story about a gymnastics meet I'd already heard. My mind wandered. I opened my book to read.

I'm not sure how long I was away but I was brought back when I heard Jen mention Halloween. She told him about the crazy time she fucked someone in error at a party. He'd been dressed as Marc Antony, just like her date, and mistaken identity had scored him her pussy. She didn't discover her mistake until later when she brought it up and her date had no idea what she was talking about. He got really angry and jealous and left her at the party alone. Jen laughed. Mark's face froze. Jen had fun with him, putting him on the spot and making him squirm.

I'll give him credit. He recovered nicely.

"No way!" he exclaimed. "Was that here on campus? I went to a costume party and the same thing happened to me. My date was dressed as Cleopatra and I thought it was her. Could that have been you? What are the odds? It's possible we've already had sex?"

Now it was Jen's turn to freeze. She had not anticipated this. She thought she'd make him uncomfortable and me too at the same time but he'd outmaneuvered her. He'd also planted the thought in Jen's mind of having sex with Mark and that was the fiendish twist I admired him for. His words would create a visual in Jen's mind and that's exactly what he wanted. Her response told me he'd succeeded.

"Um," was all she got out.

She looked so bewildered I took his side. "I guess you guys know each other better than you thought. What do you think, Jen? Does Mark look like the guy that fucked you?"

"Um, how would I know?"

Mark and I leered at her. She blushed. We'd had our fun. Time to drop it and move on.

Mark spoke, "Well, when you felt him start to cum did you tell him to give you every drop? That's what my Cleopatra told me."

What's the word for intense blushing? Jen's face and neck went crimson, and it spread all the way down to her chest.

After a moment of silence, Mark breathed, "It was you."

Now everybody knew. Mark looked at her with so much desire she couldn't meet his gaze. He wanted to eat the flesh from her bones. The sexual tension in the air was thick.

I suddenly felt strangely out of place and unsure what to do. The chemistry between these two was off the charts but Jen happened to be my girl. I loved that Mark wanted her so much and I equally loved that she wanted him, but I felt sandwiched by reality. What should I do?

"I've thought about you almost every day since that night," he said. "Even in the dark I saw how beautiful you were. Now in the light I see I was wrong; you're more beautiful than I believed. I felt a shock of electricity when I first touched you and I know you felt it too. I wanted that moment to last forever."

He was good. I remember that night he bolted as soon as he came but the feelings he described sure sounded convincing. Jen bought it completely, but then again she wanted Mark to feel this way about her. Mark's attention sent her self-esteem soaring.

This was too convoluted. Nervousness rose in me and threatened to become panic. Not only had her plan back-fired on her, mine had as well. He wooed my love right in front of my eyes and she welcomed it. I turned to Jennifer and her face was dreamy. Her rapt attention on him unnerved me. I thought about ending our get together with some bogus excuse but I wondered if she'd resist me and insist we stay. This had not gone the way I'd hoped at all. My attempt to stir things up and get Jen riled ended with me becoming the agitated one. I wanted this encounter to end. Mark saved me.

"I hate to say this," he said. "But I have to go. Jen, can I call you later? Maybe we can get a cup of coffee? What's your schedule?"

I kept my face completely under control.

"Yes, Mark, I'd love that. Let me check and I'll text you."

"That's wonderful. I look forward to it."

He packed up and shook my hand and then kissed Jen on the cheek. As soon as he was gone she melted into a puddle.

"Oh my fucking God!" she exclaimed, leaning all the way back in her chair. Her shirt was tight and stretched across her tits, accenting their large size and tear-drop shape. "Mark wants me and wants me badly. Big Man on campus can have any girl he wants and he wants me. I love it! You okay, Paul?"

"I'm good."

"You sure? You have a funny look in your eye. I'm not actually going to fuck him, Baby, I just love that he wants to so much. Ha! I win!"

"You sure loved the words that came out of his mouth."

"That's true, but what girl wouldn't? I'm with you, Honey. My heart belongs to you."

I felt mildly better. Her voice carried complete conviction.

We studied for a few hours and then hit the indoor pool. As always, I enjoyed the looks Jen got in her bikini and I know she enjoyed them too.

The next day Jen text Mark that nothing was open but she'd text him as soon as something appeared. I kept us away from the library. Mark text her every few days but Jen ignored him. She played the game and loving it. His pursuit thrilled her.

After two weeks the urge built in me again and I was ready for new slutty antics. I enjoyed her act as much as she did. I was ready for something flirtatious to happen.

I took a long hard look at myself. I loved the idea of Jen playing around but whenever things got too heated, I chickened out and back-pedaled. Afterwards I regretted my hesitation and wished I'd taken it farther. But what was the real danger? She'd been all over those guys at the pool and nothing bad came of it. Her naked pussy had actually rubbed on another guy's cock, yet here she still was my loving and devoted woman. Should I let her play around a little more? I found it exciting and so did she. What if I let it go farther?

The more I considered it the more I wanted to see. Not intercourse, but maybe something shy of that? I remembered all those pictures on her computer. Jen loved sucking cock. Could I let her do that? How would I tell her? If I did tell her, how would my suggestion make her feel?

At dinner that night I brought up Mark, asking her what her plans were regarding him; was she just going to string him along or one day just stop replying?

"Oh, I'm so glad you asked. I bumped into him at the gym today. I'm meeting him for coffee tomorrow morning at Joe's Place by the bookstore. Eight O'clock."

I played with my vegetables.

"Paul? Is that alright?"

I was torn! If I gave her permission who knows what might happen?

"So, what are your plans with him?" I asked again.

"To drink coffee and talk. To be seen in public with the hottest guy on campus. To make every girl that walks by sick with envy. What do you mean, plans? Are you jealous?"

I looked up. Her face was surprised.

"Yeah, I think I am."

Her eyes boggled. "After everything you've seen me do? The elevator? The girl at the sex show? The pool party? Oh, let's remember Mark actually fucking me while you watched. We've talked and fantasized about this so many times, Paul, why does a cup of coffee make you jealous? You confuse me."

That made sense. I decided some courage was needed.

"Because of what I've been thinking lately. Because of the way I feel."

"Go on."

I sat up straight. "Maybe a little something *should* happen between you two. Nothing major, but more than flirting. I'm sure you want to. What if I said you could?"

Her blank face was a pale circle of stone. She may have held an ace-high or she may have held a royal flush, I couldn't tell. I knew her mind moved fast.

"Paul, before you say anything else, I

want to state that fucking him is definitely out of the question. That's too far. But what are you thinking? I need to hear you say it. Can I kiss him? Can I make-out with him? Can he go down on me? Can I suck his gorgeous cock?"

I felt a little dizzy. Part of me could not believe I considered this.

"I don't know, maybe all those things. What do you think? God help me; am I being a total idiot, Jen?"

She wasn't really listening to me. Her imagination had already jumped ahead to tomorrow morning and Mark, coffee, and cock.

"No, Baby," she vaguely reassured me. "You can totally trust me. Most likely nothing will happen. It's just coffee after all, and we'll be surrounded by people."

I said nothing, somewhat regretting my words already.

After a brief mutual silence, she spoke, "You said maybe. This is exciting but a shopping list of do's and don'ts feels weird. How will I know what's okay?"

Her question sounded mostly rhetorical; I couldn't possibly name every possible scenario and give her guidelines for it. Her question also revealed she pictured them together and knew she'd want to push the envelope as far as she could.

I had a stomach full of sour bile and a heart full of angst, yet, buried down deep, some part of me wondered what she'd do. How far would my girl go? It was such a churning mix of powerful emotions I did what guys always do and shoved the whole mess aside. It was too tangled to sort.

"I leave it up to you," I answered. "I trust you."

We returned to eating and talked about mundane things. Neither of us wanted to raise the subject again. After our meal we watched Netflix and then went to bed. Jen slid down under the covers and gave me the longest, best blowjob of my life. I came so hard I almost cried. Afterwards I could not keep my eyes open and fell into a deep sleep.

We awoke together as we always do and prepared for our day. I always leave before her so rarely see that day's outfit until we meet again after school. Today she knew exactly what she wanted to wear, choosing a short black skirt that showed off her thighs and a lilac cap-sleeve top which buttoned up and billowed away from her body whenever she leaned forward. This always exposed her bra, except today, because there would be no bra. My nuts tightened once I realized she planned to show Mark her tits. They tightened again when I noticed she had no panties lying out either.

A new and very strange feeling rose in me. Every time Jen has done anything flirtatious, I've always been there to be a part of it. Today she was headed out without me. I had to trust her completely. I had to trust her love for me was stronger than her desire for Mark. It twisted my guts but also excited me.

I kissed her in the bathroom just after her shower. She stood there with a light towel wrapped around her long hair, her stunning body still wet and covered with tiny droplets. She had an aggressive look in her eye. I wanted to say something; to remind her to be good or to enjoy herself, but everything sounded either trite or insecure. Instead I just told her I loved her like I always did and kissed her again.

Class that morning was brutal. I checked my phone often but I don't know why. We'd made no plans for her to text me with updates. I watched the clock in agony as the appointed time arrived. Eight o'clock, they meet. Nine o'clock, they kiss. Ten o'clock, he's sucking her nipples and she's sucking his cock.

By eleven I'd lost my mind.

Between classes I took the long way around and walked by the coffee shop. I couldn't be positive but it looked like neither of them were there. At first I felt relief because it was over but then a wave of torment washed over me. What if they left together? Why hadn't Jen text me yet? What the fuck was happening?

I stopped and remembered to breathe. Head down, I headed for my next class.

I got home at four. Jen was already home, waiting for me in our living room, still wearing her outfit for Mark. He'd enjoyed a visual treat. I dropped my books on the kitchen counter as she walked up to me. Her arms went arms my neck and she pulled my mouth down to hers.

She'd done it!

When her tongue snaked into my

mouth, it was covered with a tart salty film. I knew instantly what it was. To my relief it tasted much better than I'd always heard.

I naturally pulled back but she held me fast. Her tongue swirled my mouth and I tasted more of him. She held me firmly until I relaxed and accepted her passionate kisses and then began returning them. We traded kisses back and forth, sharing the evidence. I tasted his cum in my mouth, smelled his pungent odor in my nostrils, felt his slick and slimy gloss across my lips. She had dried sperm crusted near one corner of her mouth and more on her cheek. Her hair was tousled and her skin and eyes glowed with vitality. She was radiantly gorgeous and sexy. Alone, my woman had sucked another man's cock and it killed me at the same time it lit me up.

A spike of panic wracked me. Had she done more? I slipped a hand under her skirt and found her sopping wet pussy. Was this more of him? I thought my heart would burst and my mind explode. Mark had fucked her!

I pushed my finger deep and she groaned.

"That should be your dick," she gasped. "I'm so fucking wet for you."

I ripped her top open and pulled her to the ground. She let me do anything I wanted and seconds later my hard penis was balls deep in her mouth, the same mouth Mark had just fucked. I couldn't wait. I pushed her back and tugged her skirt out of the way. I lined my dick up to her cunt and shoved. She cried out as I sank every inch into her steaming dripping pussy.

I knew at once he hadn't fucked her. All this soaking wetness was her desire for me and left over desire for him. I fucked her hard on our living room floor, rubbing carpet burns into both of us. I pulled out and feasted on her wet hole until she clutched my hair and cried out in orgasm. I rolled her onto her stomach and rammed my penis back in and minutes later called out her name as I whipped my penis out of her and unleashed a torrent of boiling sperm all over her back and butt.

We lay there panting like summer dogs.

When we returned to ourselves she described her morning. He was already there when she arrived at ten after eight. They talked and had a few cups and she said the sexual tension grew. When he suggested they go back to his dorm, she agreed. He's on a full athletic scholarship but has to live on campus.

She said she was on her knees seconds after he closed the door. They left their clothing scattered all over the living room, which his roommate found, and when it was time for her to leave she had to dress in front of him, but he was cute too so she liked it.

"Paul, I spent the day sucking Mark's cock again and again. His cum is the best I've tasted. He returned the oral attention and I came but I wasn't there to climax, I was there to make him climax. I wanted to drive him crazy. I wanted to be the best he's ever had."

I asked how many times she swallowed him and she did not hesitate.

"Six! I sucked him off six fucking times and swallowed every drop each time. God! Baby, he's so hot, so studly. He's such a man and that cock drives me crazy. I wanted to fuck him so much but I didn't, my love, I swear."

I pulled her down to kiss and this time actually savored his taste in her mouth. My naughty, naughty girl. My sweet cock-loving slut. She was so pretty, so sexy, so sexual. I felt like I'd won the lottery.

"Tell me more," I said.

She described his cock and balls, his hard muscular body, and what it was like to look into his big eyes and see so much desire.

"At one point I took his steel-hard erection and put it right at the entrance to my pussy. You should have seen his eyes, Baby. I was killing him! It killed me too, honestly, and I had to move it away but not before he felt how hot and wet I was for him. He asked if he should grab a condom and I told him the pussy was off-limits. He didn't ask why but he didn't like it. I saw his mind working. He grabbed my hair and forced his dick into my mouth again."

I imagined his cock mashing her small labia, the tip maybe even inside her a little, and sprouted another erection. Why did the idea excite me so much? Jen used her mouth and made quick work of my penis, smacking her lips after.

We cuddled and small-talked and

eventually got back to our life. We ate dinner and afterwards we started to watch a movie but I interrupted it when I rolled her onto her stomach again. This time I eased my dick up her asshole. Anal sex for us was exceptionally rare but Jen welcomed it. She'd been a bad, bad girl and felt deserving of anything I wanted to do to her. The more I took from her the less guilty she felt.

We showered before bed and I forced her to suck my dick again. It took me a long time to cum but Jen enjoyed the labor. I began to suspect she was probably an even bigger slut than I realized. Maybe bigger than she herself understood.

Mark text that night wanting more but she ignored him. We were both so hot and worked up by what she'd done. I couldn't get it up any more but that didn't stop her from playing with it, and our excitement carried over to the next day and the day after. All week Mark sent her texts, trying desperately to see her again, and Jen and I fucked like animals. I noticed each time he pursued her she got terribly turned-on. I knew if I heard her phone buzz there was a decent chance it was him and I was about to get my dick sucked again. Pavlov dog indeed.

Graduation approached fast. Soon I'd leave college and Jen would stay. Thank God Mark would graduate with me. I wondered if Jen would find someone to replace him. I doubted it; he had difficult criteria to match. It seemed our extracurricular sexual escapades may be coming to an end and I was surprised how disappointed that made me. Sharing her with others was excruciating but intoxicating. I hated to see it go away. I talked to her about it over dinner that night and she agreed and admitted she felt the same way. We spent a quiet and contemplative night together.

"Hey!"

The voice came at me from across the quad.

"Hey! Dude! Hang on."

I looked up to see Mark jogging towards me with six of his football buddies. Why do baseball players always seem so much smarter than football players?

"Hey," he said a third time. "Have you seen Jennifer around?"

I said I'd seen her that morning.

"Will you give her a message for me? She's not returning my calls or texts."

"Sure. Did you piss her off?"

"No, not that I know of. She came over to my place a while back and things got hot and I thought we connected but then she fell of the grid. I'd like to see her again before graduation."

Poor guy actually looked hurt. I suspected Jen had gotten to him more than he'd gotten to her. It must be killing him that he'd run into a girl that could take him or leave him. I actually felt bad for him. I suspected this had never happened to him before. There was a pain in his eyes that wasn't all bruised ego.

"Yeah, I'll tell her."

"Thanks."

We shook hands. I met his eyes and

caught a glimpse of his deep desire for my woman and at that moment decided Jen needed to fuck him before we both left school.

When we released hands we remained facing each other.

"Get rid of your posse," I stated.

He thought about asking why but something in my voice convinced him.

"Hey, guys, take off so I can talk to Paul alone. I'll catch up later."

We both watched them leave. I took a deep breath.

"I know everything," I began, "and I'm cool with it. Jen is actually my girlfriend and has been for years. One day soon I'll ask her to marry me. I apologize for the deception but she wanted it that way too. She thinks you're hot and sexy but does not want you as a boyfriend and it seems to me you are hoping for something serious with her. I don't want to play you like that. This was all about sex and just sex."

He took it well, nodding as he listened.

"I thought so," he murmured. "About you two."

"Yeah, kind of shitty but you and Jen did get to hook up some, so you can't be all mad."

He laughed. "Why tell me now?"

I took another deep breath. "Because I think you guys should fuck before we all leave school. This is a college story that would make an awesome memory. You want her and she wants you, badly, and while the idea scares me it also seems hot as fuck.

You can't have her for the long run but I have an idea and if you do what I say, you can enjoy her for a night. You in?"

Not exactly what he wanted but a hell of a consolation prize.

"I'm in."

I pulled out my phone and sent him a text.

"Come by this address tonight at nine and be ready to fuck, and I do mean fuck."

His disappointment at losing her as a girlfriend was almost wiped away by the promise of her sweet pussy. We shook hands again and I watched him walk away.

My legs were weak and my body trembled. A drop of sweat ran down my ribs. What the fuck was I doing?

Jen text me later and I told her nothing of my plan. This was my secret and my gut told me to keep it that way.

Our evening at home was uneventful except Jen let me know she was horny. Without warning I dropped to my knees behind her and pulled her panties aside. I ate her pussy from behind while she stood at the kitchen sink and washed the dishes. She was more than ready to return the favor but I told her to wait. We watched a movie and I put her hand on my erection but only allowed her that. By the time we showered for bed she craved dick.

I laid her on the bed and bound her writs to the bed frame. I did the same to her ankles. Then I blindfolded her. This was unusual but we'd done it before. I opened her bathrobe and began kissing every square centimeter of her taut and tone body. I teased her nipples and her pussy, always tightening the screws of her sexual arousal.

When the clock on the nightstand said fifteen to nine I moved between her legs and licked and sucked and nibbled her thighs and all around her pussy until she whimpered with desire.

"Paul, for God's sake, fuck me," she begged.

"Soon," I teased.

I moved to the wall unit and started some classical music before I returned between her legs. My tongue danced all around her cunt, teasing her tender flesh until she wanted to scream.

"Goddamn it! Fuck me!"

"Not yet."

I stood back. She looked incredible. Her heaving chest pushed her tits up and down. The lighting played with her tight skin, shadows showing off her strong body. She was so excited her inner labia had engorged and now peeked out between her outer labia. They begged to be touched but I resisted, instead sending my hot mouth and teasing tongue all over and around.

The clock read eight fifty-nine when I slipped off the bed and slipped on my robe. The music covered my exit.

I opened the door and Mark was already there. I silently closed the door behind him and locked it and shrugged the robe off my shoulders. He understood and stripped and I saw his body and massive cock up close for the first time. I put a finger to my lips and led him back to the bedroom.

Jen writhed on the bed, moaning, begging me to fuck her. Mark's cock rose like the head of a sea-serpent until it stood out from his body, throbbing and pointed directly at Jen. I crawled between her legs again and once more licked all around her suffering pussy.

"Please, Baby, Paul, please, I can't take any more...please."

I ignored her, of course, and continued my torment. When juices dripped from her cunt like a broken pipe, I moved back and offered her cunt to Mark. He was hard as iron and so was I. He did not check to make sure I was okay or I meant it. He crawled up between her legs on his knees and moved into a push-up position over her. He looked down to make sure his cock was lined up with her swollen slit and then he eased his cock into my girlfriend an inch at a time.

At first Jen just whimpered in relief, thrilled the teasing was over and she would get the dick she craved. Within seconds she knew something else happened.

"Paul? What, uuunnngh the fuck? Oh! Fuck. Fuckfuckfuck."

Mark eased his weight down and her pussy spread wider and wider to accept the intrusion. As each solid inch vanished inside her, Jennifer moaned louder and louder.

"Aaaaahhhh, fuck! Holy shit, Paul. What are you doing? Are you wearing a cock-ring? That feels so amazing, Baby. So good. Oh Christ! Fuck! Sooooooo good!"

Mark pushed more in and Jen's moan

turned into a squeal.

"Baby, you're gonna make me cum already. Push it all in, my Love. Give me all of it. I love it! I love it! So big! Aaaaaaaaarrrrrghhh!"

Mark still had half a cock to give her but Jen already climaxed. A drop of precum oozed from the slit in my penis. Mark held himself still and allowed Jen to cum on him and then as soon as she started to come down, buried another inch. Jen tossed her head from side to side and cried out. Another flex of his muscular ass and more of his cock disappeared inside my girl and another cry of pleasure was ripped from her throat.

At last he got the whole thing up inside her and he waited, holding most of his weight above her. She tried to touch him and wrap her legs around him but she couldn't. He left his fleshy spear buried in her guts.

When he started to move in and out he moved with excruciating slowness. Jen threw her head back and wailed at this massive insertion working her guts. Her pussy had stretched wide to engulf him and every move he made sent waves of pleasure slamming into her. Marked worked his cock in and out, gentle, tender, strong, and smooth.

I leaned forward and untied her ankles and then her wrists. Her legs came up and wrapped around his waist and her hands went immediately to her blindfold. She pushed it up and off her face.

It took her one second to focus and then she saw Mark's handsome face only inches from her own. She wrapped her arms around his neck and pulled his mouth down to hers and they kissed like Romeo and Juliette. Mark pushed every inch he had far up inside her and Jen kissed him faster and more passionately.

Jen was so wildly happy. Mark began to fuck her faster. She never looked at me. Mark slid his strong arms under her body and held her in place and then started working his huge cock in and out with increasing speed. When Jen came moments later she called out his name and begged him to fuck her all night. I moved down by the foot of the bed and the sight of his huge cock working her stunned me. His muscles curled and flexed as his python drove deep and then reappeared. Jen filled the room with cries of pleasure as he grunted and gasped.

After a while he slowed down again until his cock barely moved in and out. They kissed with lust and joy and Jen relished the sensation of a vagina and womb utterly stuffed with hot throbbing cock. Mark pushed it all the way in, struggling to get the last half-inch, flexing his ass until the entire shaft was entombed within my woman. His large testicles rested on her asshole.

He held it there and waited. The look on Jen's face conveyed some of what she felt but there was no way I could fully understand. Her eyes grew slowly larger and her mouth slowly opened. I may not understand what she felt but I understood what he did to her.

In some way only a woman could

understand, Mark overpowered her, conquered her. His massive cock resting balls-deep inside her slowly turned her from an independent, assertive woman into a submissive cock-worshiping slave. She was full of him; a man filled her completely and truly for the first time in her life. Even the tiniest movement on her part sent waves of scintillating pleasure crashing throughout her body. She tried to hold still but simply could not; her body craved it. Her mind screamed at her to give this man everything. He restricted her movement with his strength but even so she made small, humping movements. She fucked herself on his impaling cock.

When her slowly building orgasm hit, it was like nothing I'd ever even heard of. Mark seemed to know it was coming but Jen and I were caught completely unaware. His solid and enormous presence deep in the heart of her touched every place at once. As her pussy and womb began to clamp down and lock into place all around him. Her body clenched him from the inside out. Her pussy gripped his over-sized phallus in a vise until the cramping turned into pleasure and then shot through the roof as an astonishing explosion of orgasm.

Jen screamed and wiggled her hips, trying desperately to fuck herself to death on him. He kept every millimeter firmly inside her, crushing her walls, crushing her cervix, crushing her clitoris. With all her strength my girlfriend writhed up and down and around on him, fucking herself on his cock, cumming like a hurricane. She screamed again and again until he held her face to his chest to muffle her. Her pelvis twitched and convulsed. I knew he'd please her more than me but I had grossly underestimated by how much.

Mark gently kissed her face and throat as Jen's climax climbed and broke and finally began the long fall back to earth. Her breathing was ragged and water spilled from her eyes. Her body trembled. He kept his huge arms wrapped around her and his giant steel cock buried. Her nerves were frayed and any stimulation was instantly too much. She jerked and jumped from time to time.

I sat on the floor and moved my gaze to the point where their bodies merged. Jen's poor pussy was overwhelmed. His balls had drawn up tight to his body so my view was clear when he started working the shaft in and out again. It was often more than she could take and she jumped. He tenderly adjusted but kept going. She recovered quickly and soon he slid the full length in and out on every thrust.

He scooped his hands under her ass and lifted, allowing him maximum penetration. He hurt her once but she bit her lip and took it. When he went too deep again she seemed to like it. In no time he was pulling that slick pink tree trunk almost all the way out before slamming it back home again. Jen lifted her hips to meet his pounding, eager to fuck him back.

I knew what was rapidly approaching and it made my penis pulse. I should say something because at this point neither one of them would think of it, but I kept my mouth shut. Mark was about to fill her young and very fertile womb with a gallon of steaming hot sperm, something I had not done in over a year. I should not allow it to happen but God help me, I desperately wanted it to.

Mark fucked Jen, the love of my life, and the agony drove an erotic spike through my brain. I started stroking my stiff erection in time with his thrusting into my girlfriend. When Jen begged him to cum in her, I echoed her words, urging him to shoot his load deep. We all got carried away by the insanity of the moment. Mark lifted her butt even higher and drove his shank balls deep on every plunge.

"Here it comes," he loudly announced and Jen and I held our breath. "Here it comes!" he screeched again. I saw his balls lift even higher and a half second later he roared as the first white-hot blast of semen rocketed from him and deep into her. Jen sobbed and may have cum again as the spurt smashed into her womb. Mark powered his hips through another blast and then another and then he sprayed wildly inside her, pumping her full, inseminating my sweet, sweet girl. His formidable cock had swollen even thicker and was now a deep red. Again and again he tensed and ejaculated, flexed and spurt.

My mind twisted in sexual torment. My penis had never been so hard. Like him, I was now deep red and bigger. I jerked my dick fast. My first jet arched over the bed and landed on Jen's hand. I shot again and splattered our rug, again and smeared the bedspread. While Mark poured his potent baby-making sperm into Jennifer, I shot mine all over our bed and rug.

I collapsed before he did, falling onto my back and staring blankly at our ceiling. We'd done it. We'd gone all the way. Another man had fucked the love of my life. I briefly wondered what the future held but those thoughts were nudged out of my mind when I noticed my penis was still rock hard. My heart ached with what we'd done but that suffering fueled an erotic response more powerful than any I'd known.

I sat up to witness the reality of our actions and as my vision cleared the edge of our bed I saw that fat slime-covered snake stuffed into my Jen. They were still a tangle of arms and legs, kissing softly, murmuring tender words to each other as the storm of their passion drained away. The scene was pure agonizing torture. His cock was so big it dominated her. He had softened but remained stiff enough to stay inside her. His heavy member was a fleshy plug holding that enormous load of sperm inside. Her pussy held him in a loving hug, tightly gripping the instrument of so much out of this world pleasure. They lovingly kissed again.

I hadn't really thought it through when I made the decision to allow this. In the back of my mind I'd vaguely assumed Mark would fuck Jen and then leave, and then Jen and I would talk about how crazy it was. Mark and Jen had other ideas.

After ten minutes or so Mark's kisses became more aggressive and Jen responded. Mark started moving his hips and to my horror the veins on his cock grew. He grew hard again already. With her pussy now exceptionally well lubed, his tube of flesh slid in and out smoothly. Jen grunted at his deep intrusion and then lifted her hips to capture more of him. Moments later they were fucking again.

This was not my plan.

As before Mark pinned her down and she seemed to love his dominance. When we have sex it is a mutual endeavor; sometimes I lead, sometimes she does. We are partners enjoying each other as equals. With Mark, Jen became the little fawn to his grizzly bear. His overpowering masculinity allowed her to be, possibly for the first time in her life, girlie and weak. She ate it up. She reveled in it. Demure at last, Jen embraced this new side of herself, pulling her legs up and spreading them, gripping her own ankles and offering herself completely to this new man.

He accepted her offer. Mark moved his strong arms behind her knees and bent them back, causing her cunt to flower obscenely. His wide cock pushed her inner lips aside as he filled up every inch of her. Her head fell back to the pillow as she surrendered.

I'd never seen her little pussy stuffed like this. I know it is designed to stretch but to me it looked like penetration of this magnitude should hurt. The look on her face told me it was not pain she experienced at the moment.

He fucked her for almost an hour, lifting her and turning her and moving her body with the confidence of a man in charge. Jen loved it. The length of his cock allowed him to fuck her from positions I'd never even attempt. She had a leg over his shoulder when she came the first time and both her arms twisted behind her back when she came the second. As her body learned the mastery of his cock her orgasms came more frequently and also more powerfully. Sixty minutes later my sweet Jen was a boneless mass of exhausted flesh. When he filled her with a huge second load I imagined the billion possible children swimming inside her. Afterwards they lay side by side, stretched out on our bed.

Finally, Jen met my eyes.

"Come up here, Baby. Lie beside me. I want to be sandwiched between my two men."

Her words sent a blast of heat through me but I took my spot next to her. She moved us until she was a butterfly trapped in a web of male arms and legs.

We all dozed.

Jen woke me. She moved down the bed to get Mark's cock in her mouth. He still slept but she was ready for more and picked him, not me, to meet her need. She avoided my eyes as she sucked that plump head in. Mark got hard as he awoke and Jen straddled him and aimed his cock at her pussy. A heartbeat later they were fucking again, her hands on Mark's chest, her perfect tits squeezed between her elbows. The eagerness with which Jen steered that big cock back inside her took my breath away. Her fervent desire to be filled again set my heart pounding.

They fucked all night. I should have seen it coming but honestly, I didn't. My simple mind had imagined an encounter and then Jen all to myself. I'd allow them what they both so desperately craved and then he'd go away. I'd get to be the hero, the super-confident boyfriend, the awesome open-minded guy, and then Jen would love me forever.

The sun was coming up when I rolled over and whispered in Jen's ear.

"I have to go."

She nodded and kissed me several times. I could not miss class today and reluctantly slid from the bed to get dressed. Moments later I stood looking down at them. He spooned her with his soft yet beefy prick resting between her legs and pressed against her cunt. She had her body pressed firmly to his, absorbing his presence in our bed.

I closed the door behind me as I left, glancing back one last time; she was nestled against his muscular chest, his arm draped protectively across her body.

Hours later I received a text informing me he was gone, finally, and she was going to get some real sleep. I asked if they did anything after I left and after a delay she responded, "*God yes. I'll visit the pharmacy today. I love you.*"

I could imagine. A shiver ran up my

spine. I text back that I loved her too.

I understood the implications of her comment and my balls tightened and tingled. Blood rushed to my penis. I was incredibly aroused by the possibility that another man had impregnated my girlfriend, and utterly baffled by that arousal. I looked up at the white billowy clouds slowly moving across the blue sky and shook my head in disbelief.

I floated through my classes only half there. Every few minutes a scene from the night before sprang into my mind and I greeted it with either raw lust or blind panic. By day's end I was an emotional wreck and insanely horny. I raced home to Jen.

She greeted me at the door in lingerie. I don't know how she knew. She silenced me with hot kisses and pulled me to the living room floor. Our love-making was never sweeter. She considered what I'd given her a selfless act of love and felt closer to me than ever before. When it came time for me to pull out she held my butt firmly and pulled me deeper and I lost it, cumming like a geyser. Filled with two men now she was practically purring. She pulled her legs up to her chest and wrapped her arms around them. Her smile was broad and joyful. For the moment her inner-slut was content. She held Mark and me within. She carried seed from the two men in her life. She was fulfilled.

We lay together in silence a long time. Her fingers crawled across the carpet and found mine and we held hands. It felt so good. I chuckled and she did too and then we were laughing, laughing at our crazy chaotic no-rules sex life.

"What the fuck?" She said at last. "Who are we?"

I laughed again and squeezed her hand. "I thought you might enjoy that."

"You shocked the mother-fucking shit out of me, Paul. I cannot believe you actually did that. Oh-my-God. But, Baby, I'm so glad you did. That was amaaaaazing."

"Yeah, it was."

We fell silent again for a while and then she asked a question.

"What changed? Why did you do it, Paul?"

I told her about speaking to him in the quad earlier and his obviously real feelings for her. He was smitten and I felt mean. I knew she wanted it and the only barrier between them was me and after a little self-examination, I realized I wanted it too. The discovery that Mark had actual feelings for her pleased her greatly. I worried about that but soon understood it was pride and ego, not a mutual attraction.

"Now I want to fuck him again," she teased.

"Okay," I blurted, as surprised as she was I'd said it.

"Really?"

I pondered a moment, considered how I would feel after a second encounter, then a third, then a fourth. Graduation loomed on the horizon like a guillotine. Any connection they formed was doomed and that gave me security.

"Yes. There are only weeks left in the

semester and then you and I go one way and everyone else in this school go another. He'll be gone before anything can go wrong."

Her eyes beamed. I thought she was happy I'd handed her Mark again. I was wrong.

"We stay together after you graduate?"

"Of course," I answered. "No way am I letting go of you."

She squealed with joy. "You've never said that out loud," she said. "I hoped for that but a girl never knows. Oh, Baby, that makes me so happy. I love you!" She grabbed my face and kissed me.

"I love you too, Jen."

She walked to the kitchen for a glass of water and I quickly fished that tiny black box I'd been carrying around all this time. When she returned I was down on one knee, holding the box level with her belly-button. She screamed.

"What is this?"

"Jennifer Jacobs, will you make me the happiest man on earth and marry me?"

She freaked out. She sat the water down as fast as she could and flying-tackled me, knocking me backwards and kissing my face over and over and screaming yes. We kissed and hugged and cried together, happier than I ever thought I could be.

Later it occurred to me my sweet girlfriend had agreed to marry me while carrying a womb full of another man's sperm. I got so incredibly turned on I took her in the bathroom up against the mirror. It seemed somehow wrong and I had no desire to tarnish our special moment, but it sure excited me.

Jen spent the night calling family and texting girlfriends from high school and talking on the phone. I called my dad and he seemed pleased. Mom's ring looked great on her finger.

Mark is no dummy. He played his cards exactly right. He didn't call or stop by or send texts or crowd us in any way. He may not have liked it completely, but he knew where he stood, and that's why, four days later, Jen invited him back.

Jen said she wanted a threesome this time and started off sucking us both at the same time. I'm above average in size but resting in her hands like that, side-by-side and right next to her face, the difference between Mark and me astonished. I know she did not mean to but her attention was not evenly split. The longer we stood there getting our dicks sucked, the more time she spent sucking his.

She held him up to marvel at it and looked into his eyes. "You have no idea how naughty I feel just *looking* at this beautiful thing. God."

I was hurt, but only a little and it faded quickly. I watched Mark's big cock get the royal treatment and when Jen's cheeks dented as she sucked hard on the head, I bit my bottom lip and took my penis in hand, stroking with voyeuristic delight. Mark saw her new ring and told her to switch hands. I got a kick in the guts when her ring touched his cock.

Her tongue was all over him and then she'd force as many inches down her throat as she could, only to come back up for air and lovingly run her tongue from balls to slit. Once he was sloppy wet she added her hands and double stroked him while sucking and bobbing.

When Mark made sounds like he would cum soon, I impulsively nudged him out of the way telling him it was my turn.

"Her pussy needs fucking," I suggested. I was worried he'd cum in her mouth and I perversely wanted him to cum in her pussy again. To me that was the ultimate thrill. Anything else was foreplay.

Jen gave me uncertain eyes as I pushed my penis into her mouth. Mark moved around behind her and on her face I saw the moment he penetrated her.

"Baby?" she asked, keeping her voice low. "That's risky. He's not wearing- Unnnnngh! Oh, Mark, Baby, Jesus, you feel good... Paul, I'm out of- unnnnngh, fuck!"

He dropped his hands on her hips and started fucking that sweet pussy. Looking down I watched her tits wobble at every thrust. We fucked her from both ends until she screamed in orgasm around my dick. I thought about adding my load to his but I was in a mood. I fucked her mouth faster until I poured my seed down her throat and Mark exploded far up into her guts. We rested a bit and then those two went at it again. They looked amazing together; his muscular male body and her tight tone female one. I watched them move together and it was pure magic.

Over the remaining eight weeks of school, Mark fucked her six times. Twice I wasn't there when he did. I got to agonize in class after Jen sent me a text informing me she'd invited him over for some alone time with him. She was learning my buttons regarding all this stuff and having a blast with it. Once she even sent me a picture of his big hard cock resting half-way inside her. I still have that picture on my phone and I still jerk off to it.

Finals arrived and Jen and I bore down and sailed through, as usual. I had sent out resumes prior to graduation and received several interested offers and after a round of interviews, landed a nice job with Wells Fargo. Entry level, of course, but an excellent start.

Jen took the summer off and we moved to a new apartment. We established a new routine quickly; up in the morning, off to work, home, dinner, bedtime. In school she'd worked extra hard her first three years so her last two semesters would be a breeze. She'd carry a light credit load and start working part-time, whatever she could find until graduation. For now she'd see me off in the morning and spend the day reading or working out or on a million other mundane tasks until I came home. She called herself a homemaker and delighted in her new title.

Mark got drafted by the Dallas Cowboys.

My relationship with Jen was better than ever. Somehow inviting another man into our bedroom brought her closer to me. That sounds counter-intuitive but that's what happened. She also gained new respect for me. Women like confidence in a man and in her eyes I had it by the truckload. Mark was quite the catch. Jen was so impressed by me.

Our sex life was insane. Our new deeper trust fueled our intimacy and when we made love we were as close and vulnerable as two people can get. Sometimes we'd fuck. We'd draw upon our wild escapades and dirty talk drove us both crazy. We spent a lot of time in the bedroom. Or the living room. Or the kitchen.

Summer passed quickly. Between lying out by the pool and hitting the gym, Jen looked amazing. I enjoyed every head she turned and of course, so did she.

When school started our routine changed very little. One day after work we talked about her classes and she mentioned one of her professors was a handsome older man.

"Sophisticated, polished, intelligent. You know; everything girls hate."

I knew what she was really saying. Never really an issue, jealousy with Mark had diminished rapidly until vanishing completely. I quickly came to understand he did not have what Jen really needed for a relationship. She enjoyed him immensely but he was no real threat. A sophisticated, polished, and intelligent older man, was a real threat.

I looked her in the eye.

"Should I worry?" I asked.

"Probably," she taunted.

That old familiar stab of angst sliced through me.

She moved to the floor between my knees, and began unbuckling my belt.

"His name is Alex. He flirts with me every day, Paul, and I love it. Right in front of the other students, and there are some hot girls in that class. He wants only me. Does that concern you? Would you get angry with me if I fucked him? He has a nice body. Not Mark nice but lean and strong. He bicycles all over town. Great ass, too. I'd love to find out what he has hanging, if you know what I mean. He's so sexy, I'd take almost anything. He rides to campus every day and then showers. Maybe you should act like a student and wait in the locker room for him? Try to see him naked. Would you do that for your slut fiancée, Baby?"

We both knew she fucked with me but it didn't matter; it still worked. My recently freed penis rose until it waved in the air. She held her mouth over the head and breathed hot air on it.

"So, Jen, let me see if I have this right; you want me to sneak into a locker room to spy on some guy so if he looks good enough naked, you can fuck him?"

"Yes. That's what your slutty fiancée wants."

Her tongue licked the underside of the tip of my penis.

"Twisted."

"Yes," she admitted.

We both knew I'd do it even without

the blowjob tease.

She told me his schedule. Two days later after work I went by the university instead of coming home. I dropped coin in a parking meter. I used the entrance baseball players use and acted like I belonged. Everyone ignored me because I knew what I was doing.

She'd shown me his face on the school website and he was easy to find. I took a locker across from him and began undressing like I planned to workout. He kept a strict schedule so he was all business. Off came his riding helmet and shoes. I got an idea and withdrew my phone as if I'd received a text. I switched to camera mode but pretended to type. He pulled off his jersey and then pushed down his tight Lycra shorts.

A man needs a certain amount of confidence to chase a girl like Jennifer, and that's especially true of an older man. He has more to offer, mentally, but usually the body fades. What young girl wants to face a hairy beer-belly?

Alex had nothing to worry about. He may be twice my age but he was lean and strong. He either shaved or waxed as his body was utterly hairless. Incredible definition all over, I saw muscles flex and twist every time he moved. I knew Jen would find his body a delight, but I knew his cock would thrill her more. He'd just been exercising so true size was hard to tell, but regardless he still hung an above average slab of beef. He appeared to be smaller than Mark while soft, but just a little. He was also much smoother with almost no visible veins and pale pink skin. Most surprising were his testicles; his scrotum was larger and smoother than a baseball. When he looked into his locker, I silently snapped several pictures.

The hair on his head was short and grey, but he still had all of it. Even from across the gym I saw the brilliant blue of his intelligent eyes. I understood why she was drawn to him. He was cut from charismatic cloth. I started having second thoughts. If I allowed Jen to sleep with enough guys, there was a good chance she would eventually meet one more interesting and attractive than me. Why risk it?

He wrapped a towel around his waist and headed for the showers. I put my shoes and socks back on and headed for home.

Back in my car I debated a long time before I sent the pictures of that naked man to my lovely fiancée. I shook my head at our weird life. I needed to talk to her about Alex. I was intimidated and anxious. I thought about it on the drive home and realized a guy like Alex could steal Jen away. Not likely, but possible. He'd come at her from angles a guy her age could not. He'd come at her form angels I couldn't even think of, and, worse, neither could she. He'd seduced her on many levels and she wouldn't even feel it.

My phone buzzed. Jen had replied to the pics I sent.

"Oh. My. God. WANT."

Terrific. Exactly what I expected but still hard to hear.

On the drive home I reconsidered. The

more I thought about telling Jen my fears and insecurities, the less pleasant it sounded. Giving her Mark had raised my stature with her. Wouldn't running away from Alex lower it? By the time I reached home I had decided to keep my fears to myself. My gut told me trying to come between them and telling her she couldn't would only make her want him more.

A sudden insight came to me; Mark and Jen had already fucked before we ever took a step down this path. He'd accidentally fucked her but she'd stayed with me. She even loved his cock so much she'd cum on it but she still remained with me. Until this moment, I hadn't realized how much that influenced my decisions to bring them together. If I allowed it again, what harm could it cause?

Alex was totally different. Alex would be something completely new. The act would be utterly deliberate. Everything about it felt dangerous. I felt stuck; damned if I do and damned if I don't. I sighed and put my phone away. Wait and see, I guess.

For the next three days Jen greeted me at the door when I got home from work. Alex never came up. On the fourth day I came home to an empty apartment and a note stuck to the kitchen counter; *Dinner with A. Call you after.*

My stomach sank into my legs. She was with him at that moment! I forgot to breathe for about sixty seconds and then sucked huge lungsful of air. Holy fuck!

Of course I imagined him fucking her

but then I got myself under control. No way would Jen leave me a simple note if that was her plan. Still, things had a way of happening. I growled in frustration. I thought about sending a text but declined; too needy. Instead I went to the living room and switched on the Orioles game and then to the bedroom to change my clothes. My phone rang two hours and twenty-seven minutes later and I answered it with blinding speed.

"Oh! Hi, Baby," she chuckled. "How are you?"

"Conflicted. How are you?"

"Slightly drunk. Alex took me to Lawry's and I ate like a pig and drank like a fish. Now he wants to go for a drive around the lakes. Can I?"

"Has anything happened?"

"Not yet. That's why I'm calling."

Bone-chilling dread.

"What would you do if I answered no?" I asked.

"Come home and fuck your brains out."

"What would you do if I answer yes?"

She thought for a moment.

"Probably suck his cock as he drove and then come home and fuck your brains out."

I froze. I could not decide. I was so torn I was paralyzed. Jen seemed so confident.

"Paul?"

"He intimidates me," I said at last.

"You don't need to worry about him, you need to worry about me, and I can tell you there's nothing to worry about."

I exhaled. "Okay, Jen. It's up to you. Do whichever you want most."

"Thanks, Honey. You'll taste him when I get home."

The line went dead.

I sat with the dark phone to my ear for a while.

The next few hours tore me up. Alex was no Mark and I discovered that truth over and over again every fucking minute. In my heart I *knew* Jen had his cock in her mouth. I was terrified on the inside but my goddamn penis still rose to attention. I yearned to jack off but I had to save it for her. When she got home I would take my angst out on her body.

A car door closed and I peeked out the front curtain. Jen straightened her miniskirt and top and then headed for our door. I stood back. Keys, lock, Jen.

In three steps she was in my arms, lips pressed to mine. Her mouth tasted like fresh cum and I wondered how recently and how much he'd pumped in to her. I remembered his over-sized scrotum and knew those balls produced a ton of baby-batter. I found myself once again mildly disgusted and at the same time incredibly aroused at the taste of semen in my fiancée's mouth. For me, Alex shaped up to be all about conflict.

Jen had told the truth on the phone. She pulled me to the ground, freeing my penis, and sank down onto me with a pussy sopping wet. She rode me like I was there to be used and ground her hips, driving my dick as deep as possible. When she'd had enough of that she pulled off and moved her pussy up to my mouth. I tasted nothing but Jen. Relieved, I dove in and ate her like a Viking. I made her cum hard and fast. When she returned to herself so she climbed off and sucked my cum out.

"Good date?" I asked, sarcastically.

"Amazing," she responded, ignoring my wit. "He's so fucking hot. Mark I mostly just wanted to drag to bed; with Alex I want to be seen in public. *Everyone* turns to look at us and watch us. I got so much attention I felt drunk on it. We're a hot older-man younger-woman couple. I felt sexy and scandalous all night."

I dragged her to bed and the second I got hard again, I fucked her ass.

This became our routine; every few days Jen would meet Alex after school and come home to me. They always visited some five-star establishment. Sometimes they only had time or inclination to talk, sometimes they made out, sometimes she sucked his cock until he rewarded her with a massive load of white hot cum. Jen and I fucked like animals after every time she met him. I asked why he hadn't tried to fuck her yet and she had no idea.

"Is he trying to make you fall in love with him?"

Her sweet face fell. "Oh, my Baby, you're so sweet! Maybe he is but that's foolish. I talk about you all the time. He knows better."

"He knows about me?"

"Of course." She held up her ring. "He's not blind. He asked about it on our first date and I told him the truth and what he could expect."

"What did he say?"

"He likes it. He says it makes everything more exciting. He's with another man's woman and that makes everything sweeter. He's highly competitive. Everything is a conflict to him. He loves a fight."

Two weeks later Jen sat me down. The Fourth of July holiday approached and Alex wanted to fly both of them to New York for the four-day weekend.

"No," flew out of my mouth before I could stop it.

Her shoulders sagged. "I knew you'd do that."

"Jen, Honey, *four days?* Just you and him, living together, in another city?"

"What's the difference in one day at a time four times or four days in a row?"

I wanted to punch something. I doubted I'd eat or sleep the whole time she was gone.

"Something's sure to happen?"

She chuckled. "You're being unreasonable and illogical; something could happen any time I go out with him, and if it did, you'd only find out about it afterwards. Think about this, Paul. I understand your reaction but consider How many times have I already gone out with him? You have no idea what happens on those dates. You trust me then, trust me now."

I pouted.

Denial, anger, bargaining, depression, and acceptance.

Three days later I told her okay. Everything she'd said was true.

The day of her departure she wore a short denim skirt and a white peasant blouse with no bra. Her nipples were hints of darker flesh beneath a thin layer of white. She curled her long brown hair and even used a little make-up. She looked drop-dead gorgeous and tantalizingly sexy. My heart ached and my penis stiffened. Sometimes I'm so stupid. I thought she did it all for him but when I noticed the sly smile in her eyes I realized she was also trying to slay me. Mission accomplished. She had the nerve to tell me to behave while she was gone. I thought she joked until I caught her eyes. No woman on earth is a hundred percent confident. This goddess actually worried I might stray.

"Pretend I'm away on business," she suggested. "Once I graduate I may have to travel. Consider this practice."

I drank her in again. She was a nerdy sex-kitten. A genius whore. Lolita with an advanced degree. She'd haunt the dreams of every man that saw her.

A horn blared. The taxi was here. We kissed and I walked her to the door where we kissed and hugged. I watched from the living room window as Alex got out of the cab to greet her and they kissed and hugged too. My balls twitched. The cab pulled away with them.

What the fuck had I done?

My dick rose.

I stripped right there and it rose some more. Minute by minute more blood flowed in until my erection made my skin shine. My heart started thumping behind my ribs and still my penis grew harder. It started to hurt. Now deep red, the veins and arteries rose into squiggly worms up and down the length. My balls drew up tight.

Jennifer was with Alex for the next four days. She belonged to him, not me. He was her man, not me.

Clear pre-cum oozed from the slit. My hard-on raged, my emotions tumultuous. I wanted to scream and cry and smash things around me, yet my pulsing penis grew harder by the second. My spine ached trying to support my incredible lust and desire. Every second reality hammered my brain; Alex had Jen, Alex had Jen.

Why the fuck did something this painful turn me on so much?

I dropped into a chair and spread my legs as wide as possible. I'd never seen my dick look this big. I had a rampant, raging hard-on because another man possessed my woman. She'd gone to him eagerly and willingly. She wanted him.

"Fuck!" I yelled into an empty apartment. "Fuuuuuuck!"

My drop of pre-cum grew until it spilled over and ran down my now purple quivering cock. I felt the power of my dick, the palpitating *presence* of it. I wrapped my fingers gently and began to stroke. I imagined nothing sexual but instead burrowed into the storm of emotions raging inside me.

Jennifer left with Alex!

Surprisingly, it took me a long time to cum but when I did, bolts of semen flew over the back of the chair and landed like long white ropes across my chest and stomach. I came and came, crying out in sensational agony as an orgasm stronger than any I'd ever had cracked my back and twisted my arms and legs. I shot so much it ran off my torso. My hips lifted again and again as I pumped my load into an imaginary womb.

At last I fell into the chair, spent and empty.

Intense loss and loneliness rushed in and filled me from head to toe, knocking the air out of my lungs.

Jenifer left with Alex!

This was fucking agony and she'd been gone less than an hour!

The next few days I tried to stay busy. Gym, work, reading, jogging; everything failed. As soon as I could I had my penis in hand again. My orgasms were insanely powerful. I had no idea *why* this acute condition happened to me, I only knew it was. I got hard over and over again. I ached for Jen all the way through my body. I masturbated furiously all that first night and the next day. I jerked off in the bathroom at work and as soon as I got home again and every one of my orgasms was earth-shaking.

Jen sent me a text after dinner and I jumped at my phone but it was just hugs and kisses. I needed to hear her. I needed her to tell me what was happening.

But she did not.

I hated her and loved her for it. I missed her so much but I've never lived at such an elevated level of constant arousal. I wanted her to need me, to miss me too, but I also loved that the slut in her enjoyed her new man to the fullest.

On day three I was at my desk at work when my phone vibrated. I opened the message expecting more hugs and kisses but discovered a short video clip instead. I double-timed it to a stall in the men's room and hit play.

The camera angle was terrible and the filming jerked all over the place. It was so dark every image flashed by like a fuzzy smear. I saw almost nothing, until the end, and then what I did see left me stunned. I restarted it and risked a little volume but heard only heavy breathing until Alex's deep voice said, "Show him." Jen's pussy lit the screen for half a second and then the camera spun around.

A white and thinly stretched condom covered the front third of an enormous penis. He was too long for it to cover all of him. It held on to his shaft like a coat of paint, the latex pulled tight and almost see-through by his thickness. Two inches of loose rubber hung from the tip of his dick and at lease an inch of semen filled the end of the prophylactic. It looked like a small water-balloon someone had partially filled with milk.

His massive balls hung beneath his cock like twin anchors.

The screen went dark.

I looped it to play and watched it over and over, seeking new details I'd missed. I wasn't sure, but it seemed he'd not been inside Jen. Her pussy looked excited but untouched.

I wondered why she sent me this clip since it contained no sex and realized they just wanted me to see how much semen Alex produced, which was diabolical, and raise the question if they'd actually fucked yet. After three days, how could they not? They were both naked and in bed so it certainly seemed they'd crossed that line, yet he wore a condom, which meant they did not yet share real intimacy.

My heart raced and I actually smiled; Jen was as brutal as she was gorgeous. What girl sends her fiancé a video like that? This was psychological torture.

I took my erection and stroked while watching the tape. I felt mildly odd and uncomfortable staring at a man's condom-enshrouded cock while I jerked, but given the situation, it worked. I remembered her tangy kisses each time she returned home from his place. With that much to swallow, just sucking his cock probably gave her an orgasm. I bet she worked his dick feverishly, craving that flood of jizz, yearning to swallow his gushing sperm like a slut. I knew he had painted her face and body with it and more than once. I stroked my dick imagining her milking a load that size from him.

I received nothing more from them that day or the next, the infamous Day Four.

Towards the end of my work day I got a text saying they'd landed and she was on her way home and she wasn't alone. I stared a hole through the clock until I could finally leave work and race home.

I entered our dark apartment and almost tripped over the pile of luggage by the door. All the lights were off and the blinds and drapes closed. I moved quietly, which was weird because I lived here, and searched our place working towards the back bedroom.

I heard Jen moan.

I rounded the corner and there she was, on the bed, on her back, her legs straight and pointed up at the ceiling. Alex was between them, gripping her at each ankle and pushing her legs up and slightly back over her body. Her juicy cunt was a blossoming orchid, a wet and ripe target.

Alex was leisurely pumping in an out of her. Her eyes were closed and she cupped both tits, pinching the nipples. Alex saw me and grinned like a shark and pulled his cock all the way out of my fiancée.

A condom covered the front half of his fleshy weapon.

"He's here," Alex informed Jen.

His words were a prearranged signal. Jen kept her eyes closed and reached down between her legs. Her searching fingers found his latex covered erection and pinched the tip of rubber sleeve. She pulled it off. She placed fingertips along the top and bent his cock down to her pussy again. She pulled him forward with a trembling hand. His naked cock entered her and Jen loosed a sigh from way down deep. From her reaction I knew this was the first time he'd been inside her. Her mouth fell open. She'd been waiting for this a long time.

Alex began to fuck her, slowly at first but gaining speed. Mark was sometimes guilty of pounding away at Jen but not Alex. Alex was an artist. Alex used his cock to touch every sensual nerve Jen had inside her. She held herself perfectly still and savored the sensation of this man moving inside her.

Alex gazed down at her like he could not believe his good fortune. Circumstances placed this enticing young goddess beneath him, on her back with legs spread wide, and his eyes burned with fierce desire. They yearned for each other desperately.

I couldn't take my eyes off his enormous balls!

He leaned between her legs and they kissed passionately and with great familiarity. How many times had they been lovers over the last ninety-six hours? They moved together like they'd been lovers for years. Jen held his head with both hands as they made-out and Alex smoothly thrust with his hips, working her tight pussy with his thick prick. He bent down and suckled one nipple and then the other and then sent his tongue in large circles all around her firm tits. Jen arched her back to help him get his cock as deep as possible.

Alex leaned back and forced his member all the way in. My fiancée groaned and gripped his thighs. He pulled most of the way out and then drove it deep again and his scrotum slammed Jen's ass. He pushed all the way in and moved his hips, churning her guts like butter. She groaned again and her legs fell to each side, wide open and slutty.

Alex concentrated on fucking. He looked down to watch his cock move inside her pussy and I did too. He wasn't trying to make her cum at all and I suspected he'd done plenty of that over the last four days. This was all for him. He'd denied her his seed until she craved it. Now it was all she wanted. He was having fun, enjoying his little mind game, savoring the scenario he'd created to drive a dagger through my heart as he finally unloaded inside her for the first time, as she begged him for it, in our bed and in front of her fiancé.

Jen dug her heels in and lifted her hips, increasing his pleasure. She tried to push him over the edge. He sucked air and pumped faster. He was almost there. He leaned over to kiss her and before their lips met she said, "Give me every drop, Alex, Baby. I *want* it. I want it so much. Fucking fill me up."

He slammed her a few more times and then, sunk-in almost all the way, held perfectly still and let loose a roar. His giant balls lifted and fell in rapid succession as a torrent of sperm rushed up from his testicles, raced the length of his enormous cock, and burst from the buried head of his penis directly into her uterus. Milk began to drip from her pussy beneath his shaft. He drew air into his lungs and seemed to start again; once more his huge balls lifting and falling as another pint surged through him and into her. He bred her like a stud stallion. Just as his second wave began to taper off, several rapid pumps of his hips ignited a third, albeit smaller outpouring of seed and he threw his head back and bellowed again. He forced every last drop out and into her.

At last his head fell and his chin rested on his heaving chest.

His plan had been to tease my girl until she begged him to inseminate her right in front of me. He hoped to conquer us both; crushing me with despair and her with shame. What an ego maniac and wow did he ever pick the wrong couple.

He tried to look at me, no doubt to savor my agony, but Jen pulled his mouth down to hers and they kissed. He eased his hips back, withdrawing his cock, and a flood of semen followed him, gushing from her pussy and soaking our comforter. Jen's pussy was a slimy dripping mess.

That sight was one of the hottest, most erotic things I'd ever seen.

He scrutinized my face, hoping to witness my misery. I smiled. Jen and I never discussed it specifically but this was the moment we loved best. With sudden insight I realized we both wanted her filled with other men's sperm. This was the pinnacle of our debauchery; everything she did with a man was all foreplay leading us to this one ultimate moment. Dangerous, to be sure, but the absolute epitome of our scandalous escapades. Without meaning to, Alex gave us exactly what we wanted most.

He rolled onto his back lying next to Jen. His slippery cock draped over his thigh and the head almost touched the bed on the other side. She took his hand and held it. She lifted her head to smile at me. I smiled back and left the room.

I watched television out in the living room until the sounds of sex called me back again. Alex had Jen on her side with one leg up against her chest. His large scrotum rested on her thigh as he slow-fucked her and played with her tits under her arm. A light grin curled her mouth as she appreciated the full feeling his gliding penis gave her. Once again no effort went into pleasing her. Jen's orgasm was not a concern. Her purpose in life was to provide enough pleasure to the man that she forced him to ejaculate while embedded far up inside her. Jen gently rocked her hips as she clamped her vise-like vagina around him.

He didn't last long, but what man would? His penis swelled and darkened and he choked as he erupted balls deep, coughing and wheezing as his cock spit jizz. I returned to the living room.

I had dozed off when the click of the front door awoke me. Before I could move, Jen's arms snaked around my neck from either side, encircling me as she kissed my head.

"Come to bed, my Love" she murmured. I followed her down the hallway to our bedroom, the glow from the television illuminating dozens of wet streaks trailing down her inner thighs. My girl was filled to the brim with foreign seed. I was hard before I was even naked. Jen wanted me to fuck her too but I liked that only he was in there. That now familiar and welcomed agony fueled my lust as she sucked every inch of my rampant penis until I rolled her onto her stomach and once more fucked her ass. I was balls-deep when I detonated and jerked around like a man electrocuted.

We slept like the dead. She had class the next day and I had work so we didn't discuss her trip or Alex until that night. Once we did it went pretty much as I expected; he treated her like a princess, lavishing her with gifts and attention, but only allowing her to suck him. Day three he told her to milk him into the condom and send me the clip and she said once she actually saw how much he produced she died to have him inside.

"Honestly, Paul, by then my pussy suffered actual physical pain. That man is insidious. I craved him so badly the ache of my empty pussy hurt. I tried masturbating while he slept but that only made it worse. He teased me constantly. Wait until you see the clothing he bought me. I was ready to do anything he wanted but he asked me for nothing. I felt grateful he allowed me to suck his cock. Fucker."

"I think I disappointed him. He hoped I'd break down or something when I witnessed the way you gave yourself to him and then when he filled you up. Instead I loved it. Holy Christ, Jennifer, you are the sexiest woman on earth."

She giggled.

"That's what he said."

Within days we were back to our old routine; Jen stopped by his place a few times a week for wild animal sex and then came home to me for more of it. The big difference was now her pussy was awash in billions of potential babies, each one a possible little Alex. I got a special thrill when I sank my penis into her smoldering drenched cunt. I felt him all around me and when I added mine to his, my head nearly exploded. Life was great.

Alex's arrogance caught up to him, as you might expect. He started demanding more and more from Jen and she wouldn't have it. Like Mark, I think he started forming an attachment and came to see me as an intruder. She was patient with him up to a point and then she dropped the hammer and clearly let him know she chose me and wouldn't be coming back to see him. He had a perfect arrangement and fucked it up.

Work was great and school was great and our life was magical. We worked hard and pushed towards our goals and both met with one success after another. As the end of school loomed Jen started looking for a position and sent out resumes.

I brought up our wedding. We discussed things we hated and things we loved and what we both wanted. We talked about a date and the invite list.

We were lying in bed one night after making love and heading for sleep when Jen rolled over in the darkness to face me.

"Baby, after we're married, will we continue with these...exploits...of ours or will we stop once we're officially grown-ups. How do you feel?"

I thought about it a few minutes. I felt the tug towards convention and normalcy like she clearly did. It was incredibly exciting but it had risks. I imagined our life without it and a sense of loss settled over me. I asked myself if I can actually live with the torturous side of Jen taking lovers and realized I could. I actually enjoyed the torment.

"I want us to keep doing it. It's our dirty secret. We are so normal and predictable in every other way. I like that we have this dark side."

She squeezed my leg.

"I feel exactly the same way," she exhaled. "I was so afraid you'd want to stop. I would have, Baby, and never looked back. But I didn't want to."

"That's hot," I said.

She searched under the covers until she found my penis and sucked us both to sleep.

Weeks zipped by. Jen got some bites on her resumes and went to some interviews. We started making wedding plans and set a date. Jen asked her little sister to be her maid-of-honor and Tina jumped at the chance.

Ten days later there was a knock on our door and I opened it to see Tina standing on the stoop. As a surprise, her parents paid for Tina to come spend a long weekend with us to help with all the planning. The girls jumped and squealed like they'd won the lottery.

We all sat and caught up on everything that had happened since we last saw her. While they spoke to each other I ran my eyes over Tina. She had filled out beautifully and now had tits bigger than Jen. Jen was more toned and had a prettier face but Tina was gorgeous too. She wore sweats and a hoodie, just like the first time I met her, but now her body was developed enough the baggy clothing couldn't hide it.

We stayed up late and eventually I announced I had to go to bed. We showed Tina where the towels and bathrooms were and got her all set up. She wished us good night and stepped into a bathroom to brush her teeth before bed.

Jen and I got in bed, talked a little longer, and then her eyelids got so heavy we said goodnight. She was out.

I was not.

I remembered Tina from last time and the ruthless way she flirted with me. She was incredibly sexy then and she'd only gotten sexier. I heard the bathroom door open and her slippers on the kitchen floor. A click followed by a beep told me she'd turned on our computer. After ten minutes, my phone vibrated. I checked the message. Tina asked me how to print something and would I mind coming out to show her.

I checked on Jen and she was deep asleep. I slipped out of bed and moved to the door, silently closing it behind me. Adrenaline poured into my veins.

Out in the living room the lights were off and Tina sat at the desk. Her long hair was pulled back into a ponytail almost three feet long. She faced the computer but when she saw me approaching she turned in the chair to face me.

She wore a thin white V-neck T-shirt and tiny white lace panties and the glow of the computer screen cut through the fabric and showed me the under-curve of her new big tits. I smiled like no big deal and walked up to stand behind her.

"Use the book icon," I said, pointing at the screen. "Hover and then right click for the drop-down and select print."

She looked back at the screen and did as I instructed. From above and behind like this I saw her tits sticking out and straining at the cotton shirt and her strong smooth legs resting on the seat.

Fuck.

She crossed one leg up under her and that pulled her panties down and tightly over her mons. The lace turned completely see-through and I witnessed a wisp of pubic hair and the top half-inch of her slit. My mouth went dry as dust.

She asked a question about wireless systems and then another about hacking. She leaned forward on one elbow and that made the front of her shirt fall away and I gazed down at two large, smooth, perfectly shaped tits, including two delicious puffy nipples.

Fuck, fuck.

I burned that glorious sight into my memory forever and then moved to the couch off to the side. If I kept looking I'd get hard and I definitely did not want that to happen. I only had on a thin pair of sweat pants. I always sleep nude and toss these on when I leave the bedroom. If my penis grew at all the outline of it would be obvious in seconds. I needed to stay cool and calm. I sat at an angle where all Tina's talents were obstructed. We continued talking over the edge of the desk.

She put up with it for a few minutes and then took a chair opposite me. She acted utterly unaware of what she showed me but I saw the look in her eyes; she knew. This was just a girl learning her power but holy hell did she ever have strong power.

She crossed her legs and leaned back and while I no longer saw flesh, the move pulled her shirt tight across her chest revealing the shape of her tits.

We talked about school and her friends back home and dumb boys and hot girls. Tina was way ahead of her years. She stood, twisting her body so her butt faced me and then looking at me over her shoulder.

"Do I have a nice ass?"

"Okay then, good night," I replied, heading for the bedroom.

"Paul, wait, okay I'm sorry. Some guys say I do and some say I don't. Do I?"

I stopped.

"I can't have a conversation like this with you."

"Why not? You're an older man. Who

else can I talk to about this stuff? Not my parents, not other guys. Certainly not my sister. You're my sister's fiancé; I trust your opinion."

I ignored the older-man thing. "Exactly *because* I'm your sister's fiancé, silly. You are not ten. You've grown up into, into, well shit, you've just really grown up."

Her eyes flashed. I'd said something she liked very much. She straightened up and faced me. She put her hands on her hips. Good God, her body was ridiculous. Her face gorgeous. She saw me stealing glances.

"I've grown up?"

"Yes."

"You think I'm pretty?"

"I think you're gorgeous. Goddamn it, Tina, this is another conversation I can't have with you. Do you understand boundaries?"

She still had her hands on her hips when she subtly pulled her elbows behind her. This forced her chest out and pulled the shirt across her tits again.

"I saw you," she said. "You and Jen. After the funeral. You're big."

Ooooohh fuuuuck. I had to get out of here.

"No, I'm not." I tried to move passed her but she stepped over and blocked me.

"You know, I caught Jen a few times, growing up. She's naughty. She doesn't know I saw her. She loves those things and I've always wondered why. Does she suck yours a lot? I bet you guys fuck all the time."

No. No, no, no, no.

"I'm still a virgin," she continued.

"Some of my friends aren't anymore and they say it's awesome and I should do it. I look at the guys at my school and feel nothing. College guys are hot."

She stepped closer. I felt her heat on my skin. I looked down into her eyes.

"Since you won't answer me about my butt, do I have nice tits?"

She hooked an index finger at the bottom of her V-neck and pulled it away from her chest. I was now looking straight down her top at two of the nicest tits I'd ever seen. My penis twitched.

"Yes," I murmured. "Your ass is great too."

She beamed and stepped back. "Thank you."

I nodded. As I started to slip by she noticed my slightly swollen state. Fucking sweat pants showed everything.

"Did I do that?"

"Yes, of course."

"Show me."

My penis was on the way up and there was no stopping it. No way could I walk into the bedroom like this. If Jen woke I'd be a dead-man.

"You cannot touch me," I said.

"No shit. You're my sister's fiancé."

Tina crossed her arms and waited. She wanted to see my dick and she wanted to see it now. Exhibitionism doesn't usually do it for me but the idea of Tina gazing at my erection from only inches away sure did. I was hard hard hard.

I hooked my thumbs and pulled down

the front of my pants. As soon as my penis cleared the elastic it bounced up and stood proudly erect. Tina gazed at my erection from side to side and I loved it, growing harder every second. I felt guilty as fuck but definitely left it out longer than I needed to for her to get a good look. Her face was close to my dick and holy shit was that hot.

"You have a pretty cock," she stated. What's up with these Jacob girls?

"Thanks, I guess."

"Do you want me to show you something? I will. I like showing off."

"No! I mean, that's thoughtful, thank you, but I think I better get back to bed."

"Okay. Thanks for showing me how to print."

She moved aside. I shuffled back to the bedroom slowly and by the time I opened the door, I was soft again. I slipped into bed, Jen hadn't moved.

The sisters hung out a lot the first few days and I entertained myself after work. Tina dressed in sexy light dresses that Jen loved so she started dressing more feminine too.

Jen came home from school and announced the alumni football game was this weekend and she wanted to go and since this was my first year out, I agreed.

Although it was now early September, the weather was still warm and the girls dressed light. Jen had me buy one beer after another and shared them equally with Tina. We had seats on the fifty-yard line and an absolute blast screaming and jumping around as the Badgers beat LSU twenty-four to zero.

As we walked through the parking lot back to the car the girls danced a silly dance ahead of me. Jen saw a girl she knew and together she and Tina ran over to talk with her. Jen introduced me to Chris and I listened as Jen and her friend caught up. Eventually Jen asked Chris what they were hanging out for and Chris said the team usually comes out to thank the crowd after a big game.

From the corner of my eye I saw a streak of red fly passed and scoop Jen into a huge bear-hug, laughing and jumping around.

Mark.

Jen excitedly kissed his face over and over until she remembered where she was and what she did. Mark set her feet back on the ground and I shook his hand and then Jen introduced him to Tina and Chris. Tina was instantly smitten.

Mark looked great but I guess a pro workout will do that to you. Jen kept touching his arm or touching his shoulder as they talked and Tina noticed. She looked at me expecting to see jealousy and then looked confused when she found none.

I jumped into the conversation so Tina could see that Mark and I were friends too and that seemed to explain things to her. I was about to suggest we hit the road when Jen invited Mark back to our apartment with us. Tina smiled hugely and Mark asked if I was okay with it. What could I say in front of the girls? I told him of course. Jen said she'd ride with Mark to show him how to get to our new place.

We all said our goodbyes to Chris.

I don't know which made me more nervous; Jen alone with Mark or me alone with Tina. We parted company and headed for our cars.

Minutes later Tina asked, "Wow, is that Mark's car?"

We were pulling out of the parking lot and a few cars ahead of us Mark drove a jet black BMW convertible. Three cars in a row allowed him to cut in front of them.

"Yup," I drawled.

"He's hot. Did he and Jenny used to be boyfriend-girlfriend? They seem to know each other really well."

"They like each other. He was our study-buddy for years. He got drafted by the Dallas Cowboys."

"Holy shit."

"Yeah, something like that."

"I'm sure they fooled around. Before you, of course. I have to ask Jenny. He's really hot and I know all her signs. That girl can hide nothing from me. I read her like a book."

Oh boy.

We drove for a while in silence. Ahead of us Jen sat a little too close to Mark and I began to worry her head would disappear into his lap. I could not allow Tina to see that. When the opportunity came I passed them and we both waved as we went by. Sure enough, just before we lost them in the rear-view mirror I saw Jen dive out of sight. I knew she sucked his cock right now.

We got to the apartment well before them and I realized they probably stopped to finish. I started to get hard. I couldn't help it. Tina ran in to use the bathroom and I sent Jen a quick text explaining my conversation with Tina about who Mark was to us. She responded she understood and she'd let Mark know.

Once they arrived I said nothing about their delay but young Tina was less delicate.

"What happened to you guys?" she asked. "Stop for a quickie?"

"Shut up, Tee," Jen teased. "More like stopped for gas."

That worked and Tina dropped it, but I knew.

Jen handed out beers to everyone and the alcohol flowed as well as the conversation. Tina was surprisingly up on the NFL and grilled Mark about pass defenses and the New York Giants. Jen announced she would change into something more comfortable and came back out in a black tank-top two sizes too big and white short-shorts. She held back because Tina was present but not by a lot. I think she still viewed Tina as more innocent and naive than she actually was. I knew Tina would notice how much skin Jen showed and I was right.

Ten minutes later Tina made the same announcement and left to the bathroom. Jen hardly noticed. I held my breath. Sibling rivalries.

I exhaled. Tina came back wearing shorts like Jen but a full T-shirt with the sleeves cut off. Everything was covered.

Crisis averted. She sat and we all went back to talking and drinking. I noticed Mark's eyes narrow from time to time and casually turned to see why.

Every time Tina lifted her bottle to drink, the sleeve hole around her arm revealed the profile of her entire glorious breast, puffy nipple and all. I looked away. There was nothing for me to do.

Our conversation continued and Tina continued flashing Mark her tits. Eventually Jen caught on and very subtly started leaning over more and flashing Mark her tits too. After some time, Tina shifted in her seat and her shorts gaped and Mark got a nice slice of pussy lip hidden under red panties. I started to get uncomfortable. Both girls were drinking faster now too. I kept the conversation moving along.

Tina noticed the tattoo on Mark's hand and asked to see it close up. Mark extended his hand. Tina took it and rested the palm on her bare leg, high up, and Mark just leaned forward. Jen moved closer to see it too and asked him what it meant.

"It's the Celtic symbol for Warrior," he stated. "It reminds me to never give up, to keep fighting no matter what."

Tina took a huge gulp of beer. "I was thinking about a tattoo right here," she said, standing and pulling the back of her shorts low enough to partially expose her butt-crack. "I'm thinking a butterfly."

"That's a good idea, Tee," Jen said. "We should get matching tats."

She stood up and pulled her shorts

down too, several inches lower than Tina. They both giggled but left their shorts down. Tina tugged hers down lower to match Jen. Two smooth, tight, perfect asses stared right at us. These girls have had way too much to drink.

Since I was getting hard, I knew Mark was too. Mine was hidden by my baggy pants. Mark had a fat jean-covered log reaching up from his lap to his belt. He moaned playfully.

"You ladies are killing me," he said. He discreetly reached down to adjust his cramped erection. Tina bit her lip.

"Is all that *you*?" she asked, disbelieving and pointing right at his bulge.

Before he could answer Jen spoke breathlessly, "It *is* little sister. I've seen it and it's fucking beautiful. Show her, Mark."

Mark froze.

Jen did not. Down on her knees between his legs she fumbled with his belt and fly for a second and then reached in. Out came his thick turgid cock. Jen held it at the base and pushed his pants down and away, revealing his shocking erection to all. Tina whimpered, her mouth squeezed shut, and Jen grinned like the Devil. I held my breath.

Jen held out a hand and Tina joined her on the floor.

"Touch it," Jen instructed.

Tina wrapped her fingers around the shaft and Jen placed her hand on top of her sister's.

"It's hot like my curling-iron," Tina exclaimed.

Together they started stroking Mark from balls to head. He looked at me with a what-the-fuck expression but I offered him nothing. What's the protocol for cock-jacking sisters?

"Don't be afraid," Jen told Tina. "Keep stroking him like that. He likes it. You're making him feel really good." Tina nodded. Jen moved up and French-kissed Mark. Tina quickly looked at me. I shrugged. I couldn't take my eyes off her hand on his dick.

Jen rejoined Tina and again told her to keep stroking. Tina nodded again. Jen leaned forward and took the head of Mark's cock into her mouth and sucked. Mark gasped as loud as Tina. Tina jerked him into her sister's mouth. Jen pushed farther down and then sealed her lips around the shaft and sucked hard. Mark groaned.

"Oh my fucking God," he muttered. "What the fuck is happening?"

Without looking up Jen reached out and found Tina and guided her mouth down to Mark's cock too. Together they licked the upright tower and then Jen gently guided the head into Tina's waiting mouth. Mark let his head fall back. No way was he stopping this.

Tina choked and then tried again to take the cock like she'd seen Jen do. She gagged again right away. Jen pulled her off and showed her how and the Tina tried again with greater success, sucking down a solid three inches before coming back up for air, eyes watering. She dove right back down, taking four inches this time, and stayed down there bobbing her head and sucking hard.

Jen turned her attention to Mark's clothing and soon had him naked. Tina ran her eyes over his incredibly muscular body but never stopped sucking his cock. Behind Tina, Jen stood up and whipped off her tank-top and slid out of her shorts and panties. Her nipples were hard as steel and swollen with arousal to twice their usual size. She reached down and rubbed her own pussy and then stepped forward and fed Mark a tit.

Tina noticed her sister nude and quickly joined her. When Tina pulled off her T-shirt and dropped her shorts, I gasped. These two girls were a living wet dream. Tina's tits were bigger than Jen's but still held that perfect Jacob-girl tear-drop shape. She had a small downy fuzz of brown pubic hair just above her clit and two small pink pussy lips. She went right back to sucking his cock and I grasped that this might be her first cock ever. She wasn't ready to let go of it. As she sucked and licked her eyes were all over her sister's body. These two hadn't seen each other naked since childhood and yeah, a lot had changed. Tina stopped sucking long enough to tell Jen she had an amazing ass.

Jen looked down at her now naked sister and her eyes got big. She ordered Tina to stand. Tina did, turning side to side so Jen could appraise her.

"Holy shit, Tina, you're smoking hot!"

She gave her sister a playful smack on the ass. Tina squealed and then dove back on Mark's cock. Jen wanted more and put her mouth on the shaft right next to Tina's. Together they sucked every square centimeter of him. Finally, Jen needed his cock inside.

"Stand him up," she instructed and Tina held him with both hands around the base.

"Are you going to fuck him?" Tina asked, again looking for my reaction.

"Yes."

Jen climbed onto the couch and straddled his lap. Tina aimed the head at Jen's engorged slit. With one hand on Jen's ass, Tina guided Jen down until Mark's head penetrated Jen's hole. Jen sank down half-way.

"Oooohhhh, fuck, yes. God, I missed this cock."

Jen wasn't thinking clearly but Tina was and her eyes flashed over to me again. She gave me a knowing grin.

"You look so sexy, big sister. How long have you been fucking this hard dick? Hmm? How long did you have to go without when Mark moved to Dallas?"

Jen answered without thinking, "Over six months! It was awful, Tee. He feels soooo goooood."

"I bet you fucked all the time before that."

Jen lifted her hips and then sank deeper.

"Yeah, all the time. Sometimes Paul and Mark at the same time but mostly just Mark. I'm such a lucky girl. Oh! Christ, Mark! Push it all the way in, Baby."

Tina gave me a lecherous smile. "I knew it," she murmured. "Y'all are kinky."

She returned her attention to Jen and Mark. She stood behind and pushed down on Jen's shoulders, forcing more of Mark inside her sister. Jen groaned.

"Yeah, Tee, make me fuck him. I like that. Sister, you're a dirty girl just like me."

"What would momma and daddy say?"

Both girls chuckled.

"Don't kid yourself," Jen joked. "Momma is a slut too. I've seen her out when she thought I was in school and it wasn't with daddy."

Tina made an exaggerated shocked face.

Jen worked the cock with her hips and Tina continued to help get it deeper. I couldn't take any more and stripped like the rest of them. I dropped back into my chair and jerked off slowly as they played and every time Tina looked over at my hard dick, I loved it.

Jen rode Mark for a while, grinding and really enjoying his fat shaft, and then lifted off.

"Your turn, Tee."

Tina looked down at the pillar of cock jutting up from Mark's lap. It glittered like a jewel, covered with Jen's wet excitement.

"It's so big," Tina breathed.

"It sure as fuck is, but that's a good thing," Jen encouraged. "Trust me, you can take it. You'll love it after a minute. Just give it a try. This may be your first big one but I'm sure it's not your first."

I thought about saying; *Surprise! Wrong you are, Jen. I happen to know Tina is a virgin and you are about to make her lose it,* but I said nothing. Tina shot me a look to see if I was going to expose her secret but my lips were sealed. I *wanted* to see this. It was so wrong, so decadent, my dick was hard as iron. I jerked faster anticipating the moment Mark stole Tina's innocence. Tina wanted this too and was afraid if I said anything Jen would call a halt.

Tina flipped her pony-tail behind her and straddled Mark's legs. She leaned over and Mark sucked a fat tit into his mouth. Tina gasped and lowered her pussy towards that fleshy iron pole coming to get her. She bit her lip again and bent her knees and sank another two inches closer. Jen held Mark straight up and when Tina got close, reached in and spread her sister's labia. Tina, Mark, and myself all groaned simultaneously. Jen touched her sister's pussy!

Tina sank the last few inches and her little slit tried to engulf the head. The fit was incredibly tight and Tina had to relax her legs and use her body weight to force that cock up inside. It hurt her and for a second I thought she'd change her mind but she drew a breath and tried again. When the head suddenly slipped inside, she winced and softly cried out. Jen kept her spread until the first few inches were buried and then she let go to watch. Satisfied, she moved her tits up to Mark's face.

Tina took over. For a girl that never had a penis inside her before, she was amazing. Her wetness combined with her sister's provided all the lube she needed.

After just a few minutes her tiny cunt had stretched enough to take him smoothly and she lifted and dropped her pussy up and down. I'd never seen Mark this hard. His cock was an unyielding pink bar. Tina struggled to fuck it but she did fuck it, and with exuberance.

Jen moved to the floor and sucked his testicles one after the other and then licked his asshole. More than once when she came up to lick his throbbing shaft her tongue strayed and Tina jumped from the added sensation of an inadvertent tongue licking her pussy or grazing her ass. Jen was so dirty. I loved it. I worried what the morning would bring when all the alcohol had worn off, but for now anything went.

Mark stood and lifted Tina with him, keeping his cock entombed all the way to his balls. He spun to face the couch and lay Tina on it and then forced her legs far apart. God in Heaven, she looked like a sultry sexy angel. Jen climbed on the couch over her and facing Mark and offered her pussy. Mark dove in. He fucked one sister while eating the other.

After a while Jen pushed Mark out of the way and laid on top of her sister, face to face. They both giggled. Dual cunts faced Mark. The girl's tits mashed against each other and Jen gave Tina a peck on the lips and Tina brushed Jen's hair off her face.

"I can't believe this is really happening," Tina confessed.

"Me either. He's no high-school boy now is he?"

Tina shook her head. They were looking into each other's eyes when Mark pushed his cock into Jen's tight pussy. Jen moaned and Tina told her how gorgeous she looked getting fucked. Mark soon switched girls again and Jen gazed into Tina's eyes as she was fucked. After a minute or so Mark withdrew and pushed his erection up Jen's pussy once more. Lucky mother fucker. After a few minutes of fucking my fiancée he withdrew and lined up to Tina's tiny hole. Tina cried out in a mixture of pleasure and pain but told Mark to fuck her hard.

"Biggest cock you've ever had?" Jen asked.

"Only cock I've ever had," Tina replied through gritted teeth.

Jen face was pure shock.

"Mark is taking your virginity?" she squawked.

"Fuck yes he is, and he's fucking doing it right. I'll remember this night forever."

Jen was suddenly conflicted. There was no denying the erotic intensity of what we did but a protective big sister thing reared its head. Tina saw it.

"Tee, I was sure you'd done it before this."

Tina saw Jen's struggle.

"Don't you dare," she warned. Jen wrestled another thirty seconds and then decided we were way too far into this to stop. She gave Tina a quick kiss on the lips, slightly lingering this time, and looked over a shoulder at Mark.

"She's a virgin," Jen said. "Make sure

she remembers this the rest of her life."

Mark's face twisted so much I had no idea what he thought or felt, but I do know he started long-stroking Tina with his majestic cock; all the way out, all the way in. Faster and faster he went until he had Tina almost weeping from the intensity of the fucking he laid on her. Jen gazed down into her sister's eyes.

"She's almost there," Jen reported.

Mark went faster.

Tina held onto Jen's arms as disbelief spread across her face. Their nipples conducted a sword fight, tapping and dancing and flicking across each other. I had to hold back my orgasm.

"Harder," Jen instructed.

Mark pumped even faster. His hips smashed Tina again and again. He sweat now and his muscles were pumped and veiny.

"Here it comes," Jen murmured. "Make her cum. Fuck yes, Mark, fuck my little sister and make the bitch cum all over your huge cock. She'll crave big dick for the rest of her life. Just like me."

Tina arched her back and clawed Jen's arms.

"What's happening?" she yelled, panic edging her voice. "Oh my God! Jenny! Oh! Fuck! What? Ooooooooohhhh aaaaaaaarrrgghhhh!"

Tina screamed as her orgasm smashed into her and sent her reeling. She thrashed under Jen, tossing her head and clawing at the couch and Jen's back. Mark hammered away at that soft little pussy and Tina gushed juice and screamed again. Over and over Jen told her to cum, to give in to it, to let go and let her body win. Tina's climax was beautiful and erotic and terribly exciting and lasted a long, long time.

Tina's climax wound down when Mark shortened his quick thrusts and leaned over both girls, filled his lungs with air, and then roared as he began to fill Tina's pussy with sperm for the first time ever. Tina felt his internal blasts of hot semen and understanding set her blood boiling. A man ejaculated inside her! Womanly purpose exploded in her mind and another climax sent her rocketing skyward again, screaming every curse word she knew and screaming at Mark to fuck her to death, and he certainly appeared to be trying.

Mark rested on Jen as the last of his cum spurted into Tina. After a minute he pulled his wilting cock out and fell into a chair. Jen was as hot as I'd ever seen her. I had the only hard penis around so she moved into a sixty-nine with me until she came, hugging my head with her thighs and groaning. She climbed off before I could shoot into her mouth and laid on top of her sister again. She murmured so softly I couldn't hear what she said but Tina nodded from time to time. Tina looked shaken but happy.

Nobody spoke. I couldn't take my eyes of Jennifer lying naked on top of her sister.

Tina lifted her head and looked at me and then gave Jen a sly smile.

"Don't even think it," Jen replied. "No way. My fiancé, little sister? No way."

My erection ached for release. All this had been an assault on my body and my mind.

Tina rolled Jen off and slithered from the couch to Mark. She crawled across our carpet, semen dribbling from her pussy, until she nudged his knees apart and then gave his balls a nice wide lick. She draped his cock across her face and licked his balls like a dog with ice cream.

Jen walked over to them and held out both hands. "Come with me my little pretties," she cackled. Mark and I got the reference but Tina missed it. They took her hands and she led them to our bedroom.

This time I joined in but Jen made sure I knew Tina was off-limits. Too bad, but almost certainly the right move. That shit would've haunted us. All night Mark fucked both girls and I fucked Jen. Both girls sucked Mark's cock but only Jen sucked mine. Tina had gossiped with her girlfriends, of course, and thought she understood sex pretty well, but was utterly unprepared for the real thing. She'd masturbated too and thought the mild orgasm she'd experienced was what everyone was so excited about. When Mark made her cum she didn't understand what happened to her. Now she understood.

Mark was pure heroin and she wanted more and more. Even after we were all exhausted she still toyed with Mark's heavy dick. He liked it. She examined it and turned it in her hands and kissed it. For a first-timer she was a nasty girl. Runs in the family. Jen joined her and together they played with his soft spongy dick. Jen educated her.

Mark left around sunup, kissing the girls goodbye and promising to stay in touch. I had worried what would happen after the alcohol wore off but I needn't have; these girls were just as comfortable nude drunk or sober.

The ice had been broken, the taboo shattered, and for the rest of her time with us Tina rarely wore more than panties around the apartment and was often completely nude. Jen too. I think Jen also tested my loyalty and I wanted to pass.

The only real challenge came the night they had a lingerie fashion show and both girls tried on every piece of intimate attire Jen owned and then paraded around in front of me asking me to vote what looked best on each girl. The whole thing turned into a competition with each girl flirting harder and harder. When Tina hovered her slit over my erection Jen called it quits.

During the days they'd pour over bride magazines and tour the malls and make phone calls, then at night talk a hundred miles an hour about all their ideas. I stayed as engaged and involved as I could but a man has his limits.

Three nights later Mark was over again. This time I did more watching than participating and it was a voyeur's delight. Two sisters at the same time had to be a fantasy of his because his cock was a goddamn pink torpedo, a flesh-colored cannon. He was bigger and harder than I ever remembered and the girls took it as a huge compliment. He delayed his orgasm for hours and hours, providing them a massive erection to fuck from every angle and suck as long as they wanted.

With one exception the girls stayed away from each other and just enjoyed him. There was incidental contact from time to time and nobody freaked out about it but I'm such a pervert I got a rush each time it happened.

The one night something did happen was fucking amazing. Jen had been teaching Tina how to give the perfect blowjob even if the guy had a big cock. There are tricks to swallowing while still sucking without gagging and Jen knew them all. Jen had Tina get between Mark's knees and wait while Jen rode him reverse-cowgirl. Once he was close, Tina was supposed to pull his cock out of Jen and finish him off using all the tricks Jen had taught her. But that is not what happened.

Mark announced he was close and Jen leaned back out of the way. Tina tried to pull his cock out but he was too long and Jen wasn't back far enough. Tina brought her mouth closer and tried again but still couldn't so she leaned in even closer. Jen lifted higher but still not enough and when Mark announced, "now," Tina closed her mouth over what she thought would be the head of Mark's cock. Her tongue swirled and her mouth vacuumed, all like Jen had taught her, but mostly she did it to Jen's clit, as Mark was still inches inside Jen.

Jen's face was priceless.

Her little sister gave her head and she should stop it she just couldn't. It felt too good. Mark's cock popped out briefly and squirted slippery hot cum all over before Tina clamped her mouth on it and sucked down a few swallows, but then slipped him back inside Jen and reattached her mouth to Jen's clit, licking and sucking. Jennifer gazed down between her legs aghast. This was so, so wrong but Jen was about to climax. She grabbed the back of Tina's head with both hands and forced her to continue as her orgasm hit. Tina had no problem licking her sister's pussy.

The sight of Jen cumming on her sister's tongue will stay with me forever. Them too, I think. Tina didn't care at all but afterwards Jen was disturbed, although she did get over it really fast.

Hours later they tried again and this time Tina deliberately sucked Jen's pussy while Mark fucked her. My dick almost exploded. Of course Mark couldn't see exactly what happened but he had an idea and his dick pulsed and throbbed. Jen gasped when Tina's tongue first made contact and she quickly realized what Tina did. Mark held Jen's arms, trapping her, and Tina softly licked and sucked until Jen exploded, sobbing in a massive orgasm. Tina looked so pleased with herself.

We all knew now which Jacob girl was the bigger slut.

For the rest of the night Tina behaved

herself and initiated no more sex with her sister. The next day Mark flew back to Dallas and the day after that Tina went home to California. Our goodbyes at the airport were poignant and heartfelt. A new and different connection had formed between us that transcended mere family ties. We'd crossed some lines but found our way back and were stronger and more trusting because of it. My gut told me they'd never touch each other like that again but regretted nothing. The girls hugged and cried before Tina got on the plane. Neither of us wanted her to leave.

In the following days I went back to work and Jen went back to school. We worked through Christmas and New Year's, saving money and making plans.

For the first few weeks after Tina left Jen seemed self-conscious and I asked her about it. She was embarrassed about what happened between them. I said if blame landed anywhere it was on that hot little slut Tina for attacking your sweet pussy like that and we both laughed. I assured her that whole encounter had done nothing to change my mind or see her in a negative way. I suggested her and her sister's sex drive was genetic and she should relax with it. It was in the past. She smiled and agreed.

At last graduation day arrived. The family came out to see her Walk and boy were they proud. I reflected on the pronounced difference between her family and mine; she got so much support and encouragement.

Tina brought a new boyfriend along

with her, David, and he seemed like a nice guy. He was tall and lanky, with dark hair and sensitive eyes. He adored Tina, watching her constantly.

Jen graduated with honors and even gave a short speech regarding athletic achievement which the crowd loved. Alex stopped by and Jen introduced him to everyone as her favorite professor and he asked Tina if she would be following in Jen's footsteps.

"Step for step," Tina replied. Alex looked pleased. Jen and I exchanged knowing glances.

Afterwards we all went out for dinner and then her parents got a hotel room. Tina and her boyfriend wanted to stay with us. Back at our place David and I were watching a basketball game when the girls went into the bedroom and closed the door.

"Sister-stuff," they said.

Once the game ended I knocked and we both joined them, all of us talking and getting to know David better. We stayed up playing Trivial Pursuit and then crashed and slept in. Two days later Tina, David, and the parents all flew back to California.

I asked Jen what she and Tina talked about behind closed doors and she said Tina wanted a boyfriend like me; now that she'd discovered sex she wasn't about to settle on one guy and wanted to know how to turn David on to my way of seeing things. Jen gave her all the tips she could think of but mostly told Tina to talk to him and tell him what she wanted. He already liked for Tina to dress sexy and flirt with other guys and Jen thought Tina could eventually convince him to let her fuck other men, if she was patient. I smiled. David had no idea what was headed his way.

Jen got a second interview and then the job. The next year flew by faster than any year we'd known. We were so busy we had no time to look for extra fun and nothing landed in our lap so we just put our heads down and worked.

We got a stray cat, Groucho, and a Boston Terrier, Domino.

One day as we sat at breakfast our eyes met over the table and we smiled. How can life be so good? We were stupidly, deliriously happy.

"I think it's time," I said.

"I think it's time," Jen echoed.

Plans were set in motion and a date carved in stone. Six weeks from that breakfast Jen and I would be married. To help, Tina flew out fifteen days before the wedding and I got to enjoy two stunning beauties running around our apartment in panties and tiny tops for over two weeks. She brought the boyfriend David with her but two sexy sisters prancing around phased him not at all. Smart boy. Good things come to he who plays it cool.

Tina looked better than ever, which means her tits were bigger than before but her stomach was still flat and her ass still a bubble. Jen had the better body athletically. Tina was softer and more curvaceous.

One day after a shower Tina walked

from the bathroom to our bedroom and back again wearing only a tiny sheer white slip. My eyes followed her the whole way. Jen watched me watch her. Once we were alone she said, "The answer is still no and always will be, but I can't fault a man for looking. My little sis has grown into a babe. I should take her out tonight and show her off. Just the two of us, for all her hard work. We've been so stressed. We could use a nice vent."

Of course I agreed. David did too.

"Show her off" turned out to be an understatement. They stood by our front door, ready to leave, and they looked so good my male eyes ached. David could not take his eyes off Jennifer.

My fiancée wore a little black dress but under bright light it went transparent and no bra meant perfect nipple circles. Her red shoes and purse matched her red lace panties.

Tina was a little bolder. She wore a dress too but light blue and so tight it looked like a layer of paint. Bra and panties would have left unseemly lines so Tina went without either and it was so obvious. Her big tits swayed with independent motion and her nipples were hard constantly. Although large there was no sag in those beauties whatsoever. Her dress was several inches shorter than Jen's and she had David check if anything was visible when she crossed her legs. Yup. A lovely flash of pussy-slit greeted him and he told her so. David accepted her slutty side perfectly.

"Guess I better be careful then," was

all she said, changing nothing.

I kissed Jen at the door and told them both to be careful but have fun.

"Don't wait up," Jen warned. "We will be late."

"Try to text when you can," I requested. "I'll be in knots until you're both home."

The door clicked behind them and Madison, Wisconsin, swallowed them up.

Of course I fretted for the first few hours wondering about what and whom. Eventually I got over it and David and I settled into Sports Center. I received no text or call and I knew Jen enjoyed some much needed time away. I let it be. David had a harder time with it. He tried to watch television, paced for a bit, surfed the Internet, and finally came and sat before me, rubbing his nervous hands together.

"What are they doing right now?" he asked.

Of course I had no idea but that wasn't David's real question.

"Well, they might be dancing with some college guys." I watched his reaction and he seemed okay with that idea. I decided to test the waters. "Or they might be kissing some college guys; cutting loose, letting off steam." David's face did a funny dance.

"Would you get furious with Jen if she did that?" he asked.

"Nope. Jen and I have different rules. We do a lot of things pretty non-traditionally."

He struggled, torn between needing to talk to someone about Tina and his loyalty to her. I made it easy on him.

"Anything you say to me, stays with me."

He looked relieved. I waited for him to find the words.

"Tina's been hinting a lot about sex. She loves it. We make love all the time but honestly, I can't keep up. She wants to try new things. She has wild ideas and I love them but they freak me out a little too. What would people think?"

I laughed. "David, my friend, that should be your last concern. In fact, take a big black pen and cross that one off your list entirely. Fuck what people think. What do you want?"

"I don't know."

"Bullshit. You know, you're just frightened. Admit it. Say it out loud."

"I'm embarrassed."

"Here, I'll make it easy; I've watched Jen fuck someone else."

His eyes flew open.

"Really?"

"Yup."

"A man?"

I laughed. "Yes, David, a man. A man with a huge dick too. It was intense."

"That sounds exciting. I want stuff like that too and I think Tina does, but I'm afraid."

"Fear is natural but I want to hear you say it; do you want Tina to fuck another guy?"

On the spot he considered backing away but bravely stood his ground.

"Yes." A weight seemed to lift from him.

"You've thought about it? You're sure?"

"Yes. I've thought about it a lot."

"The cock is always big, right?" I asked. "Tough detail to admit to another guy but I bet I'm right. You see it in your imagination and it's a whopper; large balls, thick shaft, plump head. No doubt it's covered with veins and hard as steel and it's pounding the fuck out of your sweet little angel. She's moaning and gasping and telling you how much she loves it. Am I in the right neighborhood?"

He didn't need to answer. His face told me everything.

"None of this is news, David. I already suspected, my friend. I've seen you. You watch other men look at her and enjoy it. They went out tonight showing a lot of skin and you protested nothing. I get it. Your secret is safe. I'm a lot like you, David. You can ask me anything."

Poor kid. I'll give him credit; he got his feet under him quickly.

"When you let Jen, um, do that, were you there too?"

"Yup."

"Holy shit. What was it like?"

"Just about killed me but absolutely the hottest thing I've ever experienced. I'd do it again in a second."

He didn't need to know everything. In fact, he only needed to know some things. I'd tell him nothing about Jen and Tina or Tina and Mark.

"Did Jen ask you? How did it happen?

"Actually, I surprised her and just let another guy fuck her with me. My gut told me to do it and I was right. I knew she wanted it. The whole thing was crazy hot."

"I really want to but I'm so afraid of losing her. What if she falls in love with some super-stud?"

"Doubtful. Women use different criteria than men for choosing a partner. If Tina is into you, no man can steal her, not permanently anyway."

That last comment brought his eyes up to mine.

"Yeah, Jen got really into this one guy for about a week. Fucked him day and night. It was pure torture but it was awesome. I never seriously worried though. My heart always told me she was just enjoying the rush of a new lover. For her, I'm home."

David shivered. This was too much. I knew at that moment he pictured Tina having sex with a cock, not a man, just a big hard cock, and while he had certainly fantasized about that before, this time it was a huge step closer to reality. Add to that his beloved was out without him, doing who knows what.

"This if frightening and exciting," he admitted.

"Yes, and it only gets better from here."

He stared at the television. "So what do I do?"

"What does Tina hint about? What do you think she wants?"

"Mostly she talks about flirting and flashing but I get the impression she wants to do a lot more and only her concern for my reaction stops her."

I thought for a minute. "Send her a text? Tell her you understand how hard she's been working and the stress she's been under and give her permission to go wild?"

His hands were trembling when he pulled out his phone. He whispered, "This is crazy," but started typing. He finished and hit send. He exhaled a huge sigh and read what he'd written.

"*So I've thought a lot about your recent sex comments and I want you to know I'm in, all the way. Don't worry about me. Be as wild as you want and we'll figure it out as we go. I love you.*"

We sat in silence. I hoped Tina would text him back but there was no way of knowing. Thankfully his phone buzzed after fifteen tense minutes.

The message was from Jen and David and I watched it together. A brief video clip showed Tina in the back seat of a car, her dress pulled down from her shoulders and a Latino male between her legs and feasting on her nipple. Tina's head moved rhythmically as the man appeared to be thrusting. He looked dressed so it may have just been dry-humping but that detail was lost on David. Tina's head was back and her mouth open and her long, drawn-out moan floated from David's phone and filled our apartment.

"Holy fucking shit!" David exclaimed.

Jen's face loomed on the tiny screen and she gave us a wicked smile. "Message received and see you soon," she said. The video ended.

Almost on cue we heard feet thump the stairs outside. David and I held our breath as keys hit the lock and Jen and Tina entered with a tall, dark, and handsome Latino man. David looked like he was about to be sick.

The girls were clearly buzzed from drinking but the man seemed okay.

Jen's dress had worked up her legs and now displayed her toned thighs as she walked in with Tina behind her. Tina's dress had ridden up too but several inches higher. Every step she took flirted with a pussy-exposure. Her neckline was much lower than when she left hours ago and her throat had three fresh hickeys up high by her jaw. Her nipples were cut from diamonds and threatened to tear through the fabric of her dress.

Tina sat on David's lap as Jen came over and sat on mine. Jen introduced Lalo and he shook our hands before sitting on the couch. He had big calloused hands and a square frame body and I guessed he was a boxer or martial artist of some kind.

David noticed the hickeys and pulled Tina's hair around to cover them. Tina leaned down and kissed him deep and nasty and he returned it after a moment of hesitation. She leaned into it even more, fully aware by parting her knees she showed Lalo her up-skirt pussy. David tugged her hem down but she opened her knees wider, pushing it back up. He tugged it down again and she laughed and slid off his lap. Standing before the group, she peeled her tight dress off over her head and stood there laughing, nude except for her heels. What a fucking body.

Jen laughed too and told her that was a great idea and my fiancée left my lap to do the same thing. Three sets of male eyes ate these girls alive. The air in the room crackled with sexual tension. Jen stepped over to Tina and gave her a sisterly kiss on the cheek and then an innocent hug, mashing their boobs together.

Tina turned to David. "I really liked your text, Sugar-bear."

David gave her a nervous jerk of his chin.

"You want me to do what I *really* want to do?"

David glanced at me for moral support and cleared his throat. "Yes."

She stepped closer and kissed him slowly and softly on the lips, drawing the kiss out.

"That's sooooo hot, Sugar. That level of confidence is a huge turn-on. That makes me want to be bad for you."

She floated away from him towards Lalo. David's face slowly contorted with fear and anxiety. He loathed to watch but couldn't tear his eyes away. What would his love do? Lalo leaned back into the couch and spread his knees and Tina moved between them and started a clumsy amateur lap-dance. It didn't matter. Her body was so insanely hot and her sweet face so angelic, she could have stood there like a statue and driven us crazy.

Jen came back to my lap and I slipped an arm under and cupped her breast.

Tina started rubbing her body all over Lalo and David watched every move. Tina worked her way higher and slipped a hard nipple into Lalo's mouth. Tina moaned and then David moaned too. She heard him and smiled over her shoulder at him.

"You like that, Baby? You think I'm sexy? You like watching me with another man?"

David was paralyzed.

Tina turned her back to Lalo and sank down to sit in his lap. She opened her legs and aimed her pussy right at David but Jen and I saw too; Tina was soaked. Tina was so wet her tiny inner-lips sparkled and clung to her outer-lips. She spread her cunt with two fingers.

"Lalo turns me on, David. Should I send him home or do something about it?"

Before he answered, Tina began grinding her ass against Lalo's crotch.

David was overwhelmed. He turned his plaintive eyes to me seeking any help I could give him. I considered what I might say but Jen spoke first.

"Tell David to undress," she whispered, her voice filled with tension.

I was so surprised I laughed. "Undressed? Why?"

"Do it. Watch what happens."

I thought about it and decided maybe she knows something.

"Take your clothes off, David." I instructed.

Then I took it one step farther. "In fact, let's join the girls. You too, Lalo. I'll make the drinks. Let's all get comfortable." I stood and began undressing too.

Lalo laughed. "You guys are all crazy but what the hell, why not?"

With everyone around him nude or well on their way to being there, David grew increasingly uncomfortable. It was time to bolt for the door or join in. He moved his body like he weighed a thousand pounds but he began undressing too. When his underwear came down he was already erect.

"See?" Jen whispered. "Told you."

His penis was slightly smaller than average but incredibly hard. I saw David scan every penis in the room and concluded, correctly, his was the smallest. Guys have such a hierarchy about these things.

When Tina saw that David was hard you'd think the Pope had offered her dispensation. She got a look in her eye that said anything she wanted to do was okay.

Lalo and I were still soft but hung about the same. I was maybe an inch longer. I had him beat on washboard abs and over-all muscularity but he had me beat on raw power. His muscles were big and smooth.

He sat back down and smacked Tina lightly on her ass. She went back to the butt to crotch rub but now it was naked butt on fleshy cock.

I returned to my chair and Jen took her position on my knee. David's eyes darted all over Tina and her possible lover. His penis stuck up as he scrutinized every detail.

A hot girl like Tina giving you a lap dance will cause certain things to happen and they happened to Lalo. His penis lengthened, moving down until the skin pulled back and revealed the flared head. He may have started smaller than me but he gained fast. I caught Jen watching his cock grow and that turned me on so I started to grow too.

Lalo was now an inch longer than me and starting to rise up between Tina's legs. Jen watched his cock slowly approaching her sister's pussy and turned to kiss me.

"I can't believe what I'm seeing," she whispered. "That's my little sister. This is so indecent and lewd. I love it."

Soon Lalo's cock curled back against Tina's mons, resting in her slit, her labia hugging him on either side. He pumped his hips to slide his length up and down and sent shivers through her. She braced herself with her hands on his forearms.

Lalo kept growing. David had his eyes glued to Lalo's long cock sliding all over Tina's pussy. If Tina tilted her hips at the right moment, Lalo's cock would pierce her on the upwards thrust. I'm pretty sure David held his breath, keenly aware how every tick of the clock risked Tina's penetration. Lalo's cock was a slow piston, rising and falling and rising again.

Lalo brought his hands up Tina's succulent body, cupping her big tits as Tina began rotating her hips and grinding her cunt against his upright pole. These Jacob girls were born to fuck. Her pussy lips smeared all along the height of him.

Fully erect Lalo was bigger than me and monstrous compared to David. Tina closed her legs and gasped at the hot rigid pole she trapped. She reached a hand down and palmed the swollen head and rubbed pre-cum from the slit.

Jen was too excited to sit still so she gripped my erection and slowly stroked. Tina looked so hot leaning back on Lalo like that we just drank it in like a porno. David had a dollop of clear cum hanging from the tip of his penis and several spots on the floor beneath him. Long strands of semen hung down to the floor like fine spider webs. He was so excited he dripped, his penis drooling cum like a leaky faucet. This was killing him. His pink testicles were drawn up so tight to his body he looked like he had no balls. Tina lifted her head and scanned all of us. Her eyes were wild with desire. When she got to David she stopped and her face softened a bit. She opened her knees until her legs were wide open.

"David, Sugar-bear, I want him to fuck me, Honey. Can I?"

David's gaze darted from her face to Lalo's cock to her tits to Lalo's cock to her eyes to Lalo's cock. He was like a caged animal. He licked his dry lips. There was no point in denying his excitement. I saw the beauty of Jen's plan. David's penis looked ready to burst. His head nodded once and relief flooded Tina's face. She exhaled and relaxed.

"David, put it in me," she ordered. "I want to feel you pushing him inside. If he takes me or I give in, it doesn't count. I want you to hand me to him. Aim his cock up my cunt, Sugar-bear, for both of us."

I thought David would balk but he didn't. He left his chair and knelt right between Lalo's knees less than a foot from his cock and her pussy. His eyes ran up and down the length of that hard dick and he licked his lips again. Tina watched him and then whispered a question to Lalo. I couldn't hear them but when she looked back she told David to get Lalo's dick wet before he put it in.

"Fuck that's hot," Jen moaned.

David opened his mouth and lowered it over Lalo's cock. Tina placed a hand on the back of David's head and gently pushed down, forcing David to take more cock, then left her hand there enjoying the sensation of David's head rising and falling. Lalo's size and David's inexperience only allowed him to mouth the top two inches, but what he could suck he sucked with enthusiasm. Tina's eyes beamed with excitement. She allowed him a minute of cock-sucking and then spoke.

"That's enough. Put it in me, Baby"

David pulled his mouth away and aimed the head at Tina's slit. He rubbed the tip around, seeking her little hole, and then when he found it he pushed that dick deep. Jen and I looked at each other in amazement.

"I'm not sucking dick for you," I whispered.

"We'll see about that," she shot back with a smile. "That was fucking hot."

Lalo lifted his hips and his cock moved smoothly into Tina. He stopped for a second to adjust his feet closer and then pushed deeper. Soon only his brown balls rested outside her body. Tina played with her clit.

Tina rode Lalo reverse-cowgirl for only a short time before Lalo picked her up and moved her to the floor on all fours. He held her ass and began slow-fucking her, pushing it all the way in and holding it there for a heartbeat until dragging it out. David sat on the floor and stared at that fleshy weapon moving in and out of his girlfriend. Tina made unearthly sounds and I was as turned on by watching her fuck as I was by watching David. His face was a soap-opera. He looked at Lalo's cock with intense longing and Tina with pure adoration.

Jen couldn't take any more and climbed onto my dick and ground her pussy on me. I turned my body so we both watched her sister fuck. David started playing with his penis and when Lalo grabbed handfuls of Tina's hair and yanked, David looked ready to cum.

"You cum on Lalo's mother-fucking cock, bitch. I want to watch you cum. Fucking slut. Lalo's big dick going to make you cum big time."

Not too creative but he sure affected Tina. The more he dominated her the more excited she became. He slapped her ass and asked again if she was going to cum on his cock, then fucked her harder with it and slapped her ass and pulled her hair again.

She said yes and he pulled her hair really hard and pounded her briefly and asked again. Soon he had her saying yes over and over again until her orgasm took hold and rocked her hot little body. Lalo turned to David and grinned like an asshole, rubbing it in as Tina came all over another man's cock.

Jen wanted to cum so badly but my penis just couldn't get her there. She climbed off my lap and climbed over Tina like she mounted a tiny horse. She leaned forward, pressing her tits against Tina's back, and lifted her pussy, offering Lalo her drenched slit. He laughed and sneered at me.

"You want some Lalo cock too? Okay bitches, come get some."

He pulled out of Tina and inserted into Jen. My fiancée jumped at the thick penetration but was soon purring as Lalo pumped her. It took Jen no time to climax.

David kept watching me, seeking signs of anger or jealousy. I maintained my cool, showing him how a man shared his woman.

Jen slid off her sister to the floor and Lalo lined his erection up with Tina's cunt. He shoved it back in and started fucking her again. Tina groaned and lowered her head and tits to the floor, leaving her ass high in the air, until Lalo pounded his rod deep and shot her full. He pulled out and dropped to the floor next to Jen. Tina took the empty spot next to him.

Jen sat up a bit and told Tina to meet her at that dick and both girls soon licked and slurped Lalo's big soft member. He was no Mark and did not get hard again, but the girls didn't care. They sucked and licked his cock, passing him back and forth mouth to mouth, lifting and rolling his balls and basically making him feel like a king.

David approached Tina from behind and kissed her back. When she did nothing he moved closer and aimed his erect penis for her pussy. She turned her hips to make it easier and David breathed a sigh of relief as he sank his dick into Tina's flooded cunt. He lasted no time before adding his sperm to Lalo's. I followed his lead and did the same thing to Jen, both of us cumming as we watched our girl suck another man's cock. Of course, I had to pull out at the last second, but it was still hot.

Soon after Lalo got a call and had to leave. The four of us stayed naked and talked about the girl's night and learned they'd stumbled into a frat party. They wandered and flirted and drank and played some darts until they stumbled upon a group of young guys bragging to a group of sorority girls about how big their dicks were. Tina and Jen called their bluff and some of the guys pulled their dicks out for comparison and Lalo won. Our girls stunned them all when they left with Lalo, promising him an evening of delight.

Jen and I spent a great deal of time talking to Tina and David about their feelings. This was a major event for both of them and because we'd gone through it before we helped them understand. By the time we finished they we both ready for Tina's next fuck-adventure. We only teased David a little for sucking Lalo's dick. Jen tried to tell me next time it was my turn but I let her know that wasn't going to happen. She gave me a funny look and a smile and I knew the conversation wasn't over.

At last our wedding day arrived. Jen wore a gorgeous white dress but no bra or panties. Tina and the bride's maids wore light blue dresses and I could only guess what Tina had on under hers. As a surprise I invited Mark and Alex and they sat on my side and when Jen came walking down the aisle and saw them, I truly had a blushing bride.

End Part One

BunnyLovesBigCarrots@gmail.com

Visit my blog; MyEroticBunny.tumblr.com

Printed in Great Britain
by Amazon

17621476R00092